Rebecca wasn't sure how to answer Samuel's question. It seemed that everyone had an opinion about whether she should or not, but how did she truly feel about it?

He waited patiently for her answer. Somehow, it was easier to express her feelings under the cover of darkness. She didn't have to school her features into blankness and pretend that she was content with the way life was. It was easy to confide in Samuel. Maybe it was because he couldn't see her face.

"I don't believe I will marry. I find great satisfaction caring for the sick among us. I can be useful and I like that."

"A wife and mother does the same. There are many good men in our community."

"I find it hard to imagine someone who could make me laugh the way Walter did. It's harder still to imagine going through life with someone who doesn't make me laugh. I don't think I could abide that."

"That's understandable. You've played some good pranks yourself."

She giggled. "I'm a bully. Say it like it is."

"Okay, I agree with that."

She enjoyed his teasing. Maybe too much. This Samuel was easy to like.

After thirty-five years as a nurse, **Patricia Davids** hung up her stethoscope to become a full-time writer. She enjoys spending her free time visiting her grandchildren, doing some long-overdue yard work and traveling to research her story locations. She resides in Wichita, Kansas. Pat always enjoys hearing from her readers. You can visit her online at patriciadavids.com.

Books by Patricia Davids

Love Inspired

The Amish Bachelors

An Amish Harvest

Brides of Amish Country

An Amish Christmas
The Farmer Next Door
The Christmas Quilt
A Home for Hannah
A Hope Springs Christmas
Plain Admirer
Amish Christmas Joy
The Shepherd's Bride
The Amish Nanny
An Amish Family Christmas: A Plain Holiday
An Amish Christmas Journey
Amish Redemption

Visit the Author Profile page at Harlequin.com for more titles.

An Amish Harvest

Patricia Davids

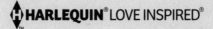

HARLEQUIN® LOVE INSPIRED®

Recycling programs
for this product may
not exist in your area.

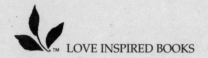 LOVE INSPIRED BOOKS

ISBN-13: 978-0-373-87967-0

An Amish Harvest

Copyright © 2015 by Patricia MacDonald

www.Harlequin.com

Printed in U.S.A.

Saying, What wilt thou that I shall do unto thee?
And he said, Lord, that I may receive my sight.
And Jesus said unto him, Receive thy sight:
thy faith hath saved thee.
—*Luke* 18:41–42

This book is lovingly dedicated
to my grandson Josh.

Of all the things in life that make it
worth living, your smile is at the top of my list.

May God bless and keep you always.

Grandma Pat

Chapter One

"**D**on't do this to me now!"

Samuel Bowman yanked his chisel away from the half-finished table leg rotating on the lathe in front of him as it spun to an untimely stop. Laying his tool aside with care that belied his frustration, he brushed away the loose ribbons of wood shavings to make sure he hadn't marred the piece. It was the last leg for a special table. An intricate piece, it had to be finished this morning if he was going to have the set completed on time.

"What's wrong, *brudder*?" Timothy, Samuel's second brother, paused on his way past. He held a cardboard box full of hand-carved wooden toys. Also a skilled woodworker, Timothy's designs were simpler and more modern than Samuel's.

"The lathe quit." A breakdown was the last thing Samuel needed. He murmured a prayer and held his breath as he flipped the machine's switch off and then back on. Nothing.

Timothy grimaced in sympathy. "Let me get these to the gift shop, and I'll take a look at it. Mother has a lady who wants to see a few more of my samples. Can't

keep the *Englisch* customers waiting. Is that the table
for the Cincinnati dealer?"

"*Ja*, and it has to be finished today. I need the lathe
working."

"Don't worry. It will all get done on time. I'll look at
it when I get back." Timothy went out the woodworking shop's front door.

It was all well and good that Timothy thought the
table would get done. He didn't have to do it. There was
more than Samuel's reputation for prompt work hanging in the balance. His father had invested the last of
the family's savings in this venture to expand their shop
and add the showroom area now packed with Samuel's
finished works. The family badly needed the money a
contract for future sales to the high-end furniture store
would generate.

Amish-made furniture was always in demand and
Samuel was one of the most skilled carvers in the area.
It was his God-given gift, and he put it to good use. Up
until now, he'd only sold his work locally from the family's gift shop. But their Amish community of Bowmans
Crossing was off the beaten path. Few tourists ventured
into the area. Samuel knew he needed to reach a bigger market if the family operation was going to expand.
With five sons and only enough farmland to support
one family, the woodworking business needed to grow,
and quickly, or his brothers would have to look elsewhere for work.

Samuel checked over every inch of the machine and
couldn't find anything wrong with it. He glanced across
the shop and spied the second of his four younger brothers stacking fresh lumber by the back door. "Luke, did
you put gas in the generator this morning?"

"I told Noah to do it."

"And did he?"

Luke shrugged. "How should I know?"

Samuel shook his head in disgust. "Why do I have to do everything myself?"

Luke tossed the last board onto the stack and slowly dusted his hands together. "Want me to go check?"

"Never mind, I don't have all day." Luke's lackadaisical offer rubbed Samuel the wrong way. Again. He loved all his brothers, but none of them had the drive that was needed to make the family business a success. Luke and Timothy would rather go out with friends than work late in the shop. Noah had his head in the clouds over a new horse. Joshua had up and married at girl from Hope Springs leaving them short a farmhand. Samuel had no time for such foolishness.

Luke hooked his thumbs in his suspenders. "When is Father going to replace that ancient piece of junk? We need one of those new diesel generators to power this place. The bishop has already said we could use it in our business."

"Our engine may be ancient, but it will last one more year and then maybe we can afford a better one. Provided you stay out of trouble. You know why father doesn't have the money to buy a new one."

Luke took a step forward, his face set in hard lines. "Because of me, is that what you're saying? He didn't have to pay for a lawyer. I had a public defender."

"That would have been okay if you hadn't pulled Joshua into trouble with you."

Luke flushed a dull red. "No matter how many times I say I'm sorry, it will never be enough for you, will it?" He turned away and stormed out of the building.

Samuel regretted his jab at Luke, but his brother's attitude irked him. It always had. He knew Luke was trying to make up for his poor choices in the past when he'd rebelled against his strict Amish upbringing and left home for the big city. He'd fallen in with bad company and ended up using and selling drugs. When their brother Joshua went to try and talk sense into him, they were both arrested and jailed. It had been a difficult time for the entire family.

Even so, it was wrong of Samuel to throw Luke's failures in his face. What was forgiven should not be mentioned again. He would find Luke and apologize later. Now he needed to get the table leg turned. He could only put out one fire at a time.

He grabbed the tool chest from the bench beside the back door in case a lack of gasoline wasn't the issue. If the generator required more than a simple fix, he wouldn't be able to finish on time, and this opportunity would pass him by.

The engine was housed in a small shed at the back of the woodworking shop. The pungent smell of exhaust filled the small room. As Samuel suspected, the fuel gauge needle sat on empty. He should have filled it himself instead of depending on someone else.

The red gas can was sitting on the floor beside the generator. He picked it up. The light weight and faint slosh revealed it was less than half-full. It would take precious time to go get more. He decided against it. Half a can would be enough to finish the job.

He opened the generator's gas cap and began pouring in the fuel. Strong fumes hit him in the face. Maybe he should've waited until the old machine cooled down a little more.

It was his last thought before a blinding flash sent him flying backward into oblivion.

"Did you hear what happened at the Bowman place?"

"I haven't. Something serious?" Rebecca Miller glanced from the cake she was slicing to her mother, Ina Fisher. Ina was putting away the goods she had picked up at the local market on her way to Rebecca's house. *Mamm* was always eager to share what news she gathered along the way when she came to visit. The Bowman family lived several miles away across the river. Rebecca seldom saw them except at church functions.

"Well, I stopped at the Bowman gift shop after I left the market this morning. I wanted some of Anna's gooseberry preserves. You know how much I like them."

"I do." Her mother's plump figure was proof that she enjoyed her sweets.

"Anyway, Verna Yoder was at the counter."

"I didn't know she worked there." Verna was her mother's dear friend and one of the biggest gossips in the county. The woman somehow knew everything about everybody. She and Rebecca's mother were birds of a feather.

"Verna doesn't actually work there. She was helping Anna for a few minutes. She told me everything. A few days ago, Samuel was putting gas in their generator for the wood shop and it exploded. His face and hands were badly burned. They aren't sure if he'll see again."

"Oh, no." Rebecca pressed a hand to her heart and uttered a silent prayer for the young man from her Amish community and for his family.

"As if that wasn't enough, the building caught fire

and a large part of their work was destroyed. They have seen many trials and tribulations in that family."

"Will he be badly scarred?" Rebecca asked, thinking of Samuel's rare smiles. He wasn't known for his sense of humor. That would be Noah, the youngest, who was the family clown. Samuel was always a serious fellow, one who seemed to study others rather than try to entertain them. She always thought his dark brown eyes looked more deeply into things than most other men.

To be blinded. How terrible for him.

"Verna only said that his face and hands are heavily bandaged. Time will tell if he is scarred. It is all in God's hands. I know his family is grateful his life was spared."

"As am I. I will pray for his healing." Rebecca didn't know Samuel well. He hadn't been among her husband's close friends, but he had made her husband's coffin in his wood shop.

She could still smell the pungent odor of the red cedar panels he chose instead of the simple white pine that was used for most Amish coffins. Walter had always loved the smell of cedar. She didn't know how Samuel knew that, but she had been grateful for the special touch even though her mother reported that some people in the church thought it was too fancy for an Amish casket.

"Verna has no idea how the family will manage. Anna is about to tear her hair out trying to run the gift shop and take care of Samuel, too. Apparently, he's a cranky patient. Harvest is coming on, and her men will soon be in the fields and won't be able to give her the help she needs. Of course, Verna heard that she sent Gemma Yoder away in tears when she tried to help."

"I wonder why?"

"That Gemma has had her sights set on Samuel for ages, but I can't see her being much help in the sickroom. The girl cries at the drop of a hat."

"What is the church doing to help?" Rebecca knew their community would rally around the Bowman family.

"A group of men have volunteered to repair the building, but Isaac won't let them start until everyone is finished with their harvest or the weather puts a stop to the field work. I'm sure the church will take up a collection to help cover his medical expenses next Sunday."

Rebecca's finances were meager, but she would give what she could. "What else can we do to help?"

"Why don't we each fix a meal and take it over. That would lighten Anna's burden."

"That's a fine idea. I'll make up a casserole and bake another carrot cake for dessert." She finished slicing the one in front of her and slid two pieces onto the white plates she had waiting. She carried them to the table where her mother joined her. Her mother stopped in to visit every Tuesday afternoon, and Rebecca always made something special to share with her.

Her mother smiled and took a seat. She forked a bite into her mouth and sighed. "I like your carrot cake almost as much as I like Anna's gooseberry preserves. It's too bad the Lord gave Anna all sons and left her without daughters to help in the house. And such troublesome boys, too. I remember how humiliated she was when Luke and Joshua were arrested on drug charges. My heart ached for her. I don't know how she bore it."

"Joshua was wrongly accused."

Mother pointed a finger at Rebecca. "But Luke

wasn't. An Amish fellow selling drugs, what is the world coming to?" She clasped her hand to her chest and shook her head making the ribbons of her white *kapp* jiggle.

Rebecca chose to ignore her mother's dramatic flair. "Luke repented and has remained a solid member of the church. We should not speak harshly of him."

Her mother's lower lip turned down in a pout. She stabbed her fork into her cake. "I wasn't speaking harshly. I was merely stating a fact."

"Joshua married a lovely girl last month. Surely his wife is helping Anna."

"They are still away on their wedding trip. Anna has two sisters near Arthur, Illinois. The newlyweds are staying with them and visiting cousins in the area. Anna wrote and told them not to cut their visit short. Verna thinks it was a foolish thing to say. I agree."

Rebecca thought back to her own wedding trip. She cherished every moment of the time she and Walter spent getting to know each other's families. Her marriage might have been short, but it had been sweet. Tears pricked the back of her eyes, but she blinked them away. He was only out of her sight for a little while. Someday, they would be together again in Heaven. Until then, she would live her life as God willed.

"I saw John at the market. He asked about you." The tone of her mother's voice changed ever so slightly.

Rebecca braced herself for the coming conversation. "How is my brother-in-law?"

"Lonely."

A twinge of pity pushed Rebecca's defenses lower. "He told you that?"

"He didn't have to say it. It was easy to see. His

wife has been gone for three years. He has to be lonely. You're lonely, too. You try to hide it from me, but I'm not blind. I don't know why you won't consider marrying John. Everyone in his family is for it."

Rebecca concentrated on her cake. "It's barely been two years since Walter died. I know everyone thinks it's a good idea, but I'm not ready." Would she ever be?

Her mother reached across the table and covered Rebecca's hand with her own. "Walter loved you. He loved his brother. He would want to see you both happy."

How could she be happy with someone other than her beloved? He was the yardstick by which she measured every man. None could come close to the sweet kindness in his voice, the tender touch of his hand, the sparkle that sprang to his eyes each time he caught sight of her. No one could replace him, but her mother was right about one thing. The loneliness was sometimes hard to bear.

"Walter would want to see you holding a babe of your own. Don't let your sadness rob you of that joy. You aren't getting any younger."

"I'm only twenty-five. I've got time." Rebecca's dreams of a family had died with Walter. She mourned that loss almost as much as she mourned her husband. If only they had been blessed with a child, then she would have been able to keep a part of Walter close to her heart and she wouldn't be so alone.

Her mother sat back and picked up her fork again. "Time has a way of slipping by us unnoticed, Rebecca. Don't throw this chance away. Give John some encouragement. You could have children of your own, companionship, security. I don't want you to be alone all your life."

Was her mother right? Should she consider remarrying, if not for love, for the blessings a family would bring?

Rebecca studied the cake in front of her. She did want children. She liked John, but was that enough? Could she grow to love him in time? Not as she had loved Walter, of course, but enough to be content in her later years?

"I'll think about it." That would satisfy her mother and allow Rebecca to change the painful subject.

"*Goot.* I've invited him and his folks for supper on Sunday after church services. I'm sure the two of you can find a few minutes alone. Are you still working for the Stutzman family?"

Rebecca shook her head as much at her mother's blatant attempt to manipulate her as to answer her question. "*Nee*, Mrs. Stutzman's mother arrived to help with the children and the new baby. I'm unemployed again."

She wasn't a trained nurse, but her experience caring for her husband during his long illness had taught her a great deal. She put that knowledge to use helping others in the community such as new mothers or those with infirm elderly family members who required extra attention. Sometimes an English family would hire her, too. It wasn't steady work, but she found it rewarding. It kept the loneliness at bay and kept her from being a burden on her mother or the church community. She knew they would provide for her, but she hated accepting help when she was able to work.

"So you will be home now."

Rebecca nodded. "Until I find another job."

"*Goot*, you are free to visit with John whenever he wants. I'll let him know."

Rebecca closed her eyes. "*Mamm*, don't pester the man."

"He's always happy to hear from me. You wouldn't need to work at all if you married again. John makes a nice living as a farrier. His first wife never complained."

Rebecca cast her mother a beseeching glance. "I'm sure a horseshoer in an Amish community earns a decent wage. Can we drop the subject now?"

Her mother shrugged. "I don't know why you are so touchy about it. You're going to let a good man slip out of your grasp if you aren't careful. I'm simply trying to steer you in the right direction."

Rebecca was saved from replying by the arrival of a horse and buggy that pulled up to the gate outside. The interruption was welcome. "I wonder who that is?"

"I'm sure I don't know who it could be."

Her mother's feigned innocence caused Rebecca to look at her sharply. "Did you invite John over today?"

"It's no sin to be friendly."

Rebecca cringed inside, braced for an awkward afternoon and then opened the door. But it wasn't her brother-in-law. Isaac Bowman stood hat in hand on her small front porch.

He nodded to her. "*Goot* day, Rebecca. I hope I haven't come at a bad time."

She stepped back. "Not at all. Won't you come in, Isaac? My mother and I were just enjoying some cake and coffee. Would you care to join us?"

"I'd rather say what I've come to say and not waste time."

Rebecca stepped out onto the porch with him. "As you please. I've only just heard about Samuel. I'm very sorry."

"*Danki.* That is why I've come. I want to offer you a job. My wife needs a live-in helper until Samuel recovers. She is having trouble managing the store and the house with him abed. Noah normally works in the store in the afternoons but I'll need all my sons in the fields when we start harvesting."

"Can't you close the store for a time? I'm sure your customers will understand. Or hire someone to work in it for your wife."

"I could, but I'd rather not. You will think I'm cruel, but my wife needs to get away from Samuel. Away from thinking she must do everything for him. I know you took care of Emil Troyer before he passed away. The old man was blind, so you have had some experience with a sightless person. Please say you will help us, at least through the corn harvest. Anna won't listen to me, but she knows you have experience with sick folks. She might listen to you. If you can't help, maybe you could suggest someone else."

Rebecca glanced over her shoulder. Her mother was scowling and shaking her head. If only her mother hadn't latched on to the idea of pushing John and her together. Rebecca didn't want to spend the next days and weeks thinking of excuses to avoid him. A new job was exactly what she needed. She graced Isaac with a heartfelt smile. "I can start today if you don't mind waiting while I gather a few things."

His expression flashed from shocked to pleased. "I don't mind at all. *Danki*, Rebecca. You are an answer to my prayers."

Samuel waited impatiently for his brother to adjust the pillows behind him. As usual, Luke was moving with the speed of cold molasses. With his eyes covered by thick dressings, Samuel had to depend on his hearing to tell him what was going on around him. Maybe forever.

If he didn't regain his sight, his days as a master carver were over. He wouldn't be of any use in the fields. He wouldn't be much use to anyone.

He refused to let his thoughts go down that road. He prayed for healing, but it was hard to seek favor from God when he had no idea why God had visited this burden on him. He heard Luke shaking the pillows and then finally felt him slide them into place.

"There. How's that?"

Samuel leaned back. It wasn't any better, but he didn't say that. It wasn't Luke's fault that he was still in pain and that his eyes felt as if they were filled with dry sand. After six days, Samuel was sick and tired of being in bed and no amount of pillow fluffing would change that, but he didn't feel like stumbling around in front of people looking hideous, either. Only his mouth had been left free of bandages. He chose to stay in bed to avoid having others see him like this, but he didn't have to like it.

He licked his swollen and cracked lips, thankful that he could speak. The doctor thought he must have thrown up his hands and that protected his lower face to a small degree. "It's fine. Is there water handy?"

"Sure."

Something poked his tender lip. He jerked away.

"Sorry," Luke said. "Here is your water."

Samuel opened his mouth and closed it around the drinking straw when he felt it on his tongue. He took a few long swallows and turned his head aside. He was helpless as a baby and growing weaker by the day. His legs and his back ached from being in bed, but he didn't want to blunder around the room and risk hurting his hands in another fall. One was enough.

Luke put the glass on the bedside table. "Is there anything else I can do for you? Do you want me to fluff the pillows under your hands?"

Before Samuel could answer, Luke pulled the support from beneath his right arm. Intense pain shot from Samuel's his fingertips to his elbow. He sucked in a harsh breath through clenched teeth.

"Sorry. I'm so sorry." Luke gently placed Samuel's bandaged hand back on the pillow. "Did that hurt?"

Samuel panted and willed the agony to subside. The pain was never gone, but it could die down to a manageable level if he was still. "I don't need anything else."

"Are you sure?" Luke asked.

"I'm sure," Samuel snapped. He just wanted to be left alone. He wanted to see. He wanted to be whole. He wanted the pain to stop.

He caught the sound of hoofbeats outside his open bedroom window and the crunch of buggy tires on the gravel. His father must be home. A few minutes later, he heard the outside door open and his mother's voice. She must have closed the store early.

"*Mamm* is back." The relief in Luke's voice was almost comical except Samuel was far from laughing. He heard his brother's footsteps retreat across the room. At least he was safe from Luke's help for a little while. Their mother was a much better caretaker. She could be smothering at times, but her heart was in the right place. Like a child afraid of the dark, he found her voice soothing and her hands comforting.

An itch formed in the middle of Samuel's back. With both hands swaddled in thick bandages, he couldn't reach to scratch it. He tried rubbing against the pillow, but it didn't help. "Luke, wait."

His brother's footsteps were already fading as he raced downstairs. Samuel tried to ignore the pricking sensation, but it only grew worse. "Luke! *Mamm!* Can someone come here?"

It seemed like an eternity, but he finally heard his mother's voice from the foot of the stairs. "I'm here, Samuel, and I've brought someone to see you."

He groaned as he heard the stairs creak. The last thing he wanted was company. "I'm not up to having visitors."

"Then it's a pity I've come all this way." The woman's voice was low, musical and faintly amused. He had no idea who she was.

Chapter Two

Samuel cringed. He hated people seeing him this way. Was this another gawker like the last girl who had come to help? All Gemma Yoder could do was sob at the sight of his bandages and burned peeling skin. She'd been worse than no help at all. Thankfully, his mother had quickly sent her packing.

"It's Rebecca Miller," his mother said. He could tell she wasn't pleased.

He heard them move closer. He knew the name even if he didn't know the woman well. "Walter Miller's widow?"

"*Ja.* Walter was my husband." The tone of her voice changed slightly. Samuel sensed the loss beneath her words. Why would she visit him? They barely knew each other. She wasn't one of his mother's friends. It was common for Amish neighbors to help each other, but she didn't live close by.

"Thank you for coming, but as I said, I'm not up to company."

"I can see that. Why are you still in bed?"

"He's in bed because he was badly burned. I'm sure

my husband told you that," his mother chided. "Samuel, your father has hired Rebecca to help us for the next few weeks."

No wonder she was upset. He had overheard her telling his father that she didn't need or want someone to help with his care after the last woman left. His father rarely went against his wife's wishes. Why this time? Samuel rubbed his back against the pillow still trying to ease that itch. "I'm glad you will have help in the store."

He caught a whiff of a fresh scent that reminded him of spring flowers. Amish women didn't wear perfume, so perhaps it was the shampoo she used. His sense of smell had become more acute since the accident. Whatever it was, he liked the delicate fragrance, but he didn't like visitors.

"Lean forward." When she spoke, she was close beside him.

"Why?"

"Because I said so."

That was bossy. He did as she said and was immediately rewarded by her fingers scratching the exact spot that had been driving him crazy. How did she know?

"I'm not familiar with what it takes to run a store, but I do know how to care for sick people. You should be up and out of bed unless you want to end up with pneumonia on top of everything else. Anna, you know this. Why are you letting him be so lazy?"

Her mild scolding annoyed him. "I'm not steady on my feet. Mother knows that."

"Ah, the explosion addled your brain," Rebecca said as if discovering something important.

"My brain is fine. It's my eyes and my hands that were injured. I can't catch myself if I start to fall."

"Rebecca, Samuel needs constant care. He will be up when he's ready." He felt his mother smooth the covers over his feet and tuck them in.

"He won't ever be ready if you coddle him, Anna."

"She isn't coddling me," he snapped. He couldn't see. He couldn't use his hands. He needed help with everything. Couldn't she see that for herself?

"Then you should move downstairs so your mother doesn't have to run up here every time you call. You aren't trying to make things more difficult for her, are you?"

"He's not making things difficult for me," his mother said quickly. "I don't know why my husband thinks I need help. I'm managing fine."

"Hello? Is anyone about? Anna, is the store open?" a woman's voice called from downstairs.

"*Ja*, we are open. Just a moment," his mother answered.

"Go on, Anna. I can manage here. Samuel, do you need your mother to do anything for you before she leaves?" Rebecca's voice was so sweet he could almost hear the honey dripping from her tongue."

"*Nee*, I don't need anything at the moment," he said through clenched teeth. If she was trying to be annoying, she was doing a fine job.

"Excellent. You see, Anna, Samuel and I will rub along well together. Don't keep your customer waiting. I'll sit with him until you come back. He and I need to get better acquainted, anyway."

Rebecca hadn't expected it to hit her so hard.

Stepping through Samuel's doorway was like stepping back in time. All her previous patients had been elderly folks or new mothers. Not since her husband's death had she taken care of a grown man in the prime of his life. Memories flooded her mind pulling her spirit low. Day after day, she had watched Walter grow weaker and less interested in what went on around him and more dependent on her. She willingly became his crutch, not realizing the damage she caused until it was too late.

Rebecca struggled to hide her dismay at the sight of Samuel. She had forgotten how much he resembled Walter. They were of the same height. They had the same broad shoulders and straight golden brown hair cut in the familiar Amish bowl hairstyle. Could she do this? Could she be a better nurse to Samuel than she had been to her dear Walter?

God had placed this challenge in her path. It was a test of her strength and her faith. She would not waver but stand firm and do her best. Even if the patient didn't like what she had to do.

She made shooing motions with her hands to get Anna moving. She knew she was being hard on Samuel and his mother, but after listening to Isaac on the buggy ride here, she already understood some of the family's problems. Samuel's mother was smothering him with kindness.

While Rebecca felt sorry for Samuel, more sympathy wouldn't do him any good. Isaac had expressed his concerns about Samuel's state of mind. Samuel wasn't getting up. He wasn't trying to do things for himself. It was so unlike Samuel that no one knew what to do. Luke and Noah both felt guilty about the accident. They blamed themselves for not taking better care of the equipment. They were trying their best to make it up to Samuel.

His mother had taken to treating him like a child instead of a grown man. The more she did for Samuel, the less he did for himself.

Rebecca's husband had been a strong man suddenly struck down with a heart attack at the age of thirty-five. It left him weak, unable to work his land and feeling useless. It took a long time for her to understand what was wrong with him, why he wouldn't try to get better. He had simply given up and eventually his damaged heart failed him.

That wasn't going to happen to Samuel, no matter what outcome he faced. With God's help, she was going to make a difference this time. Samuel needed to be shocked out of his complacency and self-pity. Thankfully, Isaac had had the good sense to hire her.

She was embarrassed to admit how fast she had jumped at his offer. Isaac hadn't even had a chance to mention her salary before she told him she could start. He had agreed to her usual wage without comment, clearly relieved she was willing to take on the job.

The same could not be said for her mother.

Rebecca put that conversation out of her mind and sincerely hoped her mother and John were having a pleasant visit at her home. No doubt, she would be the primary topic of their conversation, but she was here in this house for a reason. Anna Bowman wasn't going to release the reins of her son's care easily. Rebecca braced herself for the coming battle.

"It's a beautiful day outside. Why don't you go sit on the front porch and enjoy it. This nice fall weather won't last long."

"I'm fine where I am."

"You may be fine, but trust me when I tell you these sheets need to be laundered."

"They're fine. Go away."

"I'm not going anywhere. Your father hired me to do a job."

"What job? Annoying me?"

"If that's what it takes to get you better, I will do it gladly. Come on, up you go." She flipped the covers back. He wore blue-striped pajamas. He curled his bare toes and crossed his burned arms gingerly. "I'm not going anywhere."

"All right. I guess I shall have to wash these sheets with you in them." She picked up the glass of water beside the bed and poured some on his feet.

"Are you crazy?" Samuel jerked his foot away from the cold liquid. Had she just poured water on his bedding? The woman was off in the head.

"Now the sheets are wet so you'll have to get up."

"I can't believe you would do such a thing to a sick man. Where is my father? If he hired you, he can fire you."

"You are injured—you aren't sick. There's nothing wrong with your feet and legs. I do understand that even simple tasks are now a challenge, but hiding in bed is not the answer. Swing your legs over the side and sit up for a few minutes. Don't stand too quickly, and you won't get dizzy."

"What choice do I have?" He rubbed his foot on his pajama leg to dry it.

"Several. You can stay in your damp bed."

He didn't respond.

"Not to your liking? All right. You could yell for

your brothers or father to come and escort me home. I'm sure your brothers won't think less of you for letting a woman get the upper hand and having to rescue you from my clutches. Shall I go get one of them for you?"

He would never hear the end of it. "Leave them be. They have work to do."

"*Goot.* I'm glad to hear you say that. So do I. I'm going to move your legs to the side of the bed."

"I can do it." He didn't wait for her help. He swung his feet off the bed and used his elbows to push himself into a sitting position. He kept his hands raised so he wouldn't bump them.

She touched his shoulder. "Are you dizzy?"

"A little." He hated to admit it.

"Take some deep breaths."

He did and the wooziness passed.

"Now, I'm going to keep hold of your elbow while you stand."

"What if I fall?"

"I'll try not to trip over you while I'm making your bed."

He wasn't amused. "Very funny."

"I thought so."

"I'm serious. I could fall and hurt you."

"You could, but you won't. If you start feeling weak, I'll have a chair right behind you."

He heard her drag the ladder-back chair that sat at his desk closer. "Are you ready?"

"Will you pour water on my head if I say I'm not?"

"*Nee*, I would not want to get your bandages wet. However, I notice you don't have any dressings on your back."

His father was going to have to get rid of this woman.

"What kind of nurse would pour cold water down her patient's back?"

"One who is tired of waiting for her patient to get out of bed!"

He rose to his feet, fully expecting to pitch forward on his face the way he had the first time he'd tried to stand by himself. It had been agony getting up and back into bed without help. He never wanted to feel so helpless and alone again.

"Very good. Take two paces forward and then turn left. The doorway will be directly in front of you."

With her firm grip on his elbow to guide him, he managed half a dozen steps, but his hands were starting to throb and his legs were growing weaker. He held his hands higher. The thought of descending the stairs without being able to see made his legs shake. Fear sent cold shivers crawling down his spine.

"That's enough for now," she said. "Go ahead and sit down. The chair is right behind you."

He had to trust her. His knees gave way. He sat abruptly, but the chair was in the right spot. At least he wasn't lying facedown on the floor.

"Raise your hands a little higher. I'm going to pile some pillows on your lap so you can rest your arms on them."

He braced for the ordeal, but she handled his burned hands with gentleness, arranging the pillows at the perfect height for his comfort. "You did very well, Samuel."

Was that praise from her? *"Danki."*

"Will you be all right here for a few minutes?"

Her tone was definitely kinder. She had a pleasant voice when she wasn't ordering him around or poking fun at him. "I'll be fine. Close the window. I don't like the draft."

She began humming as she closed the window. It was an old hymn, one he liked. He heard her pulling the sheets off the bed and bundling them together. She was still humming as she carried them out of the room. The sounds of her light footsteps on the stairs faded and he was alone.

He shifted in the chair. He was comfortable enough. It was better than lying down. Not that he would admit as much to Rebecca Miller. He wiggled his toes and then lifted his legs, first one then the other. How had they become so weak so quickly? He kept working them until he heard her coming up the stairs.

"I'm back."

"I can hear you."

"It won't take me a minute to remake the bed if you're tired."

"The mattress is wet. You can't expect me to sleep in a soggy bed."

"I barely got the linens damp. The mattress is fine, but I'll flip it over if it makes you feel better."

"There's no need if it isn't wet."

"Okay." She continued humming. The flap of the sheets told him she was making his bed. He heard the slight sound of her hands smoothing the fabric into place. The flowery scent was stronger now.

"What is that smell?"

"Lavender. I sprinkle lavender water on the sheets before I iron them. It keeps them fresh-smelling a lot longer. Is it bothering you?"

He took a deep breath. "*Nee*, it smells good."

"I grow lavender in my garden and I make it into

soaps, oils and sachets. It's a very beneficial plant and it has so many uses. It's soothing on the sheets and the scent can help some people sleep better."

She stopped talking. He sensed that she was standing beside him. He tipped his head away from her. "Do you have a glass of water in your hand?"

"Why? Are you thirsty?" She was trying to keep her voice even, but he heard the humor lurking underneath. She was laughing at him.

"I was afraid you'd think I need a bath."

"You do."

He hadn't had one since before the accident. Maybe it was past time. He'd have Timothy help him with that this evening. He was the only one of Samuel's brothers with enough patience and the ability to work in silence. Samuel quickly changed the subject. "Do you sell your homemade soaps?"

"*Nee*, I give them away to family and friends."

"You should consider selling some in our store. The *Englisch* love Amish-made stuff and they pay well for things like my mother's jams and jellies."

"I'll think about it. I could certainly use some extra income. Are you ready to get back in bed?"

Was he? Not really. It wasn't bad being up as long as he wasn't alone. "I might sit here awhile longer."

Rebecca allowed her smile of triumph to widen. She knew he would feel better once he was up. "All right. I'm going downstairs and start supper."

"You're leaving?" The touch of panic in his voice surprised her.

"I'm only going downstairs. I will hear you if you call. What would you like for supper?"

"Some of *Mamm's* chicken broth will be okay. I'm not fond of the beef broth."

Her mouth dropped open. "Is that all you've been eating? Broth?"

He shifted uneasily in his chair. "My face hurts. I can't use my hands. *Mamm* figured out that something I can sip through a straw works best."

"No wonder you're so weak. I need to get some real food into you."

"I'm not going to have someone spoon-feed me. Especially you."

"That sounds like pride. Our faith teaches us to put aside all pride and be humble before God. Are you a prideful man, Samuel?"

She waited, but he didn't answer. "I didn't hear what you said," she prompted.

"I'm not prideful," he answered softly, but with an edge of irritation.

"Of course not. I'm sorry I misunderstood. Please forgive me. If you're okay in the chair, I'm going to get the wash started and then supper. Which one of your family members shall I ask to help you with your meal and your bath?"

"Timothy. But I'm not coming downstairs to eat."

"That's fine. Just call if you need me."

She crossed the room to the door, but didn't leave. Instead, she waited and watched.

He turned his head to the side as if listening for her. After a long minute, he muttered, "Fat chance I'll ask her for help."

She smiled. He wasn't sure she had gone. He was testing to see if she was still about. He kept his head cocked with one ear toward the door. She silently slipped out, taking care to avoid the squeaking stair treads she had noted on the way up.

Rebecca was used to finding her way around strange kitchens. A quick check of the refrigerator and the pantry gave her the fixing for a hearty chicken and noodle casserole. That would be easy for Samuel to eat and filling for the rest of the family. After putting the chicken on to boil, she started the laundry in the propane-powered washer in the basement, swept the kitchen and washed the kitchen floor. While she worked, she kept an ear out for any sounds from Samuel's room. She was prepared for his call, but not for the loud thud that shook the ceiling above her.

She dashed up the stairs and found him sitting on the floor at the foot of the bed. There was blood on the bandage covering his left hand. She rushed to his side. "Samuel Bowman, what have you done to yourself?"

Samuel gritted his teeth against the unbearable pain in his hands. He couldn't breathe let alone answer her.

"Are you hurt anywhere else?" Her voice penetrated the fog in his brain.

"Why? Isn't this bad enough? Maybe I can break a leg. Would that make you happy?"

"I'm sorry you're hurting, but that's not an excuse to be rude."

The pain receded, but his humiliation grew by leaps and bounds. This was exactly what he had been afraid would happen. Hitting the floor hurt every bit as much as he knew it would.

This was her fault. "Why didn't you come back? You said you only be gone for a little bit. I was stuck in that chair for ages."

"I'm sorry about that. Forgive me. I thought you would call for me when you were ready to go back to bed. Let me help you up. Do you think you can stand, or should I fetch your father or one of your brothers?"

"I can do it. Get out of my way."

"Very well."

He heard her move aside. He gathered his legs under him and lurched to his feet. He would've fallen again if she hadn't stepped in front of him and placed her hands on his chest.

"I've got you. Relax. Take a deep breath. Get your bearings."

He tried, but it was hard to do with a woman holding him up. The flowery fragrance was from her hair. The top of her head came to his chin. Was her hair blond or pale brown? He couldn't recall. He remembered her pale face streaked with tears at her husband's funeral and the flash of gratitude in her eyes when she noticed the cedar panels in Walter's coffin, but Samuel wasn't sure if her eyes were blue or gray.

"Are you steady now?" She stepped back but kept a firm grip on his arms.

He was dizzy, but he wasn't about to admit it to her. His hands still smarted. "I'm fine."

"You could've fooled me."

"This is funny to you, isn't it?"

There was a slight pause, then she said, "Maybe just a little. The bed is four steps to your left."

Determined not to give her anything else to laugh at, he shuffled in the direction of the bed until he felt the mattress against his leg. He sat down with a sigh. Gingerly lowering himself onto his side, he raised his feet. She was there helping lift them and slipping them under the covers.

"I hope you have learned your lesson," she said sternly.

Was she really going to lecture him? "What lesson would that be?"

"It is less painful to ask for help."

"It would've been less painful if I had stayed in bed in the first place."

"I can see you are a glass half-empty kind of fellow. We will work on that."

"I'm not sure I will survive any more of your lessons."

"Why didn't you call for me?"

"Why didn't you return?"

"I didn't realize how stubborn you are. I won't make that mistake again."

"Not with me you won't. As soon as my father comes in, he will take you home."

"Something you don't realize is how stubborn I can be, too. I'm not going anywhere. Your mother needs help. Whether you believe that or not. I am here to help her by looking after you. We got off to a bad start, Samuel. Let's try to get along."

"A bad start? You poured water on my sheets."

"Only because you wouldn't do as I asked. In the future, we will both have a better understanding of our limits."

"Don't get comfortable here. You'll be leaving."

"Oh, ye of little faith. It's time for your pain pill. According to your father, the doctor wants you taking them every four to six hours. I'm sure you must need one now."

He did, but he hated to admit it so he kept silent. She returned a few moments later and said, "Open wide."

He did need something for the pain. Reluctantly, he opened his mouth and swallowed the pill with a long drink of water from the straw she held for him. *"Danki."*

"I'm going to mark on your bandage with an ink pen. I promise to be careful."

"Why?"

"I need to make sure the bleeding has stopped."

"I'm bleeding?"

"Only a small amount through the bandages on your left hand. If I mark the edge of the bloodstain, then I can check in a little while and make sure it isn't getting bigger."

He braced himself for the task, but she completed it without hurting him. She straightened the bed and turned his pillow. The fresh coolness against his neck helped ease his tension.

"I'm going downstairs now. If you need anything, you can call for me, or you can make a loud thump on the floor again, whichever you prefer."

"Nice to know you enjoyed seeing me fall on my face."

"Actually, I didn't get to see it. Give me some warning next time so I don't miss it again."

"Are you deliberately trying to make me angry?"

"Are you deliberately trying to make me out to be a cruel shrew?"

"I didn't say you were cruel."

"Oh, just a shrew."

"You're twisting my words!"

He heard her approach the bed. "Samuel, you will be

fine in a very short time. I know it doesn't feel like it now, but you will. This road to recovery is painful and frustrating, but it has an end. Your mother needs help and I need the job. Let's not fight. If we carry on like this in public people will think we're married."

"We wouldn't want people to think that."

"Exactly."

He hadn't considered that she needed work. She was a widow and dependent on others for her livelihood. His conscience smote him. The Lord compelled men of faith to care for widows and orphans. "I can be civil if you can."

"*Goot.* We'll get along fine, Sammy, as long as you do what I say."

Just when he thought she was being sensible. "It's Samuel. We'll get along fine, *Becky*, if you listen to what I think before you decide what's best for me."

"Very well, we have a deal. You won't regret it."

Had he just agreed to her staying?

Chapter Three

Rebecca almost laughed when Samuel opened his mouth to protest but snapped it shut again. He wasn't used to losing arguments. He was a man used to getting his own way.

Goot. He needed to find that inner strength again. If irritation with her brought it to life that was fine. He would most likely speak with his father later, but for now, she had the upper hand. But the upper hand wasn't what she was here for. She was here to help him get better and to cope with his injuries.

Maybe she should try seeing things from his perspective. Taking care of Emil Troyer had taught her a lot about the ways blind people coped. She closed her eyes, turned around once and tried to cross the room without losing her sense of balance. She quickly became disoriented. No wonder Samuel was insecure and fearful. Without the use of his hands to feel his way around, he was twice as blind. His fall had reinforced his belief that he needed to stay in bed. It was a setback to be sure, but she wasn't willing to let him.

She had an idea. "How are your elbows?"

"What kind of question is that?"

"Are your elbows burned like your hands? Are they bandaged? I can't tell under your pajama sleeves."

"My elbows are fine. So are my knees. Would you like to see me crawl on them?"

"Maybe later." She crossed to the wall and tried using her elbows to help keep her balance and find her way. As she suspected, keeping one elbow or her shoulder in contact with the wall made moving easier.

"You are nuts," Samuel muttered.

She ignored his comment and returned to his bedside. "I'm going to suggest that you keep one elbow against the wall when you move around the room. It will help you maintain your balance and give you something to lean on if you feel dizzy. It won't help you cross an open room, but it will allow you to get up and move around without someone with you."

"I'm not going to be moving around my room."

"Of course you will be. Several times a day, in fact, but you've done enough for today. I'll bring your supper up after your brother has helped you bathe."

"You are not going to spoon-feed me," he muttered.

Her resolve weakened in the face of his embarrassment. It had to be hard to depend on others for every aspect of his care. It must be doubly humiliating to have a strange woman telling him what to do. Still, she was here to do a job and that job was to get Samuel well. Coddling wouldn't help him.

"Would you rather lick it off the plate like a dog? I guess that will work, but it might get the bandages on your face dirty not to mention my clean sheets. If that's the plan, I'll have your brother wait until after supper to bathe you."

"Go away. You're making me crazy."

That was better. There was more life in his voice. "I'm going. All you have to do is ask. Verna Yoder was right for a change. You are a cranky patient."

"I haven't spoken a word to Verna Yoder. Why would she say I'm cranky? And why are you gossiping about me? Who else is gossiping about me?"

"Samuel, you know full well if Verna Yoder is talking about you, *everyone* has heard what she has to say. The woman would gossip with a tree stump."

"She would be cranky, too, if she'd been through what I've been through."

"On that we can agree. She isn't one to suffer in silence. But, we shouldn't speak disparagingly of her. She is a member of our church and we must accept her, flaws and all, as a child of God. I'm sorry for my unkind thoughts, as I'm sure you are, too."

"I'll keep my thoughts to myself so you can't share them with Verna and who knows who else."

She laughed outright. "Smart man."

A grunt was his only reply.

She softened her tone. "Do not fear. I will spread the word that you are a *wunderbarr* patient, Samuel. Easy to care for and sweet natured. Everyone will know you as kind and good-natured with never a cross word to be said about anyone."

A twitch at the corner of his mouth could have been a smile. "Then you'll be guilty of lying."

"I think not. Is there anything you need before I go finish the laundry?"

"My eyesight restored."

She heard the fear underlying his words even as he

tried to make a joke out of it. "If God wills it, Samuel, it shall happen. Many people are praying for you."

"We both know prayers aren't always answered."

A stab of familiar pain took her breath away. Her prayers for Walter's recovery had gone unanswered, but in the last days of his illness, she finally understood that she had been praying for the wrong thing. "Our prayers are answered if we ask to humbly accept God's will, Samuel."

"I'm not sure I can do that. Not until I understand why this happened to me."

She understood his despair and confusion. He felt betrayed. She had, too. "Why did He call my husband home so soon? I have no answer for that or for your injury. We must not question His will. We must accept that His plan is greater than we can see."

"Since I can't see at all, that won't be hard."

He was determined to look on the gloomy side of things. She would tolerate that for a while, but not for long. "God was merciful to you, Samuel. I'm surprised you don't see that. Your clothes didn't catch fire. You could have been burned everywhere."

"I had a large leather apron on over my clothes and wide leather cuffs over my sleeves to keep them from getting caught in the lathe. They protected my arms and body. I don't know that God was looking out for me."

"How can you say that? Who prompted you to put on your apron and cuffs that morning? I am sorry this happened to you, Samuel. I can't begin to imagine what it must be like. I'm sure the pain is hard to bear, but not knowing if you will see again must be deeply frightening."

* * *

Samuel pressed his lips tightly together. He didn't want to talk about fear or the future. Changing the subject, he said, "I'm sorry you lost your husband."

Rebecca was quiet for a long moment. Then she said, *"Danki."*

Samuel heard the tightness in her voice. So it was still hard for her to speak about Walter. She must have loved him very much. Samuel didn't want to feel sorry for her, but he did.

"I never thanked you for adding the cedar panels to Walter's coffin. It was a kind touch. How did you know he liked the smell of cedarwood?"

"I once saw him admiring a cedar trinket box at our shop. He kept opening it and inhaling with a funny little smile on his face."

"I love the smell of cedar, too. It had a special meaning for us. Did he buy the box?"

"He didn't, but he told me he might be back for it. Later that same day, a tourist stopped in and purchased it. Walter came back the next day and I had to tell him it was gone. I made another one but he never came back to the shop. I learned later that he had taken sick. I should have brought it by the house, but I didn't."

Had Walter been planning to buy it for her? Samuel wanted to ask what special meaning the scent held for them, but decided against it. It was much too personal a question. He didn't want to start liking this bossy tyrant. He didn't want to hear about her feelings for her husband, or how she survived his loss. He just wanted to be left alone with his own misery. "I'm tired now."

"I understand. Do you need anything before I go?"

As soon as she spoke, he realized he didn't want her

to leave. He wanted her company for a while longer. Her voice was pleasant when she wasn't ordering him around or poking fun at him. Companionship wasn't something he'd needed before. He worked best alone. He preferred it to having to watch others who couldn't do a task as well or as quickly as he could. People frustrated him. His brothers frustrated him. Rebecca frustrated him. He didn't like that he wanted her around.

"I'm fine. Peace and quiet, that's all I ask," he snapped.

"I'll be downstairs if you need me, Samuel," she said gently. It was an unspoken rebuke for his churlish attitude. And deserved.

"I know. Call or fall on the floor to get your attention, whichever I prefer."

She laughed. "Something along those lines."

After she left his room, the sound of her laughter stayed in his mind. She had a pretty laugh. Not horsey or simpering. Rebecca Miller laughed like someone who enjoyed life. His grudging smile pulled at the bandages on his face and made him wince.

His grin faded. Rebecca had faced great sorrow. How did she find the strength to be happy? He shared the same Amish faith she did. Was her faith stronger than his was? Or was she a stronger person? Was it true that she didn't question God's plan for her life? He had a hard time believing that. How could she not? No husband, no children. Her future must look bleak at times. As did his when he found the courage to think about it.

Samuel listened for her throughout the next hour or so. He had no way of telling time. The days and nights tended to crawl by with nothing to do but feel pain. Rebecca kept humming or singing softly so he knew where she was. When he heard the washing machine running in the basement, he sat up gingerly on the side of his bed. His mother had an ancient wringer washer that his father had adapted to run off propane. Samuel knew Rebecca would be down there feeding the clothes through the wringer for a while. Standing slowly, he moved up the bed until his elbow touched the wall by his headboard.

Although he was still unsure of his balance, he discovered he wasn't afraid of falling on his face as long as he had the wall to lean on. He made one slow circuit of the room. He remembered the chest beneath the window in time to avoid stubbing his toe on it, but knocked his shin against the leg of his desk. It was a minor discomfort compared to his previous fall. How much damage had he inflicted on his burned hands?

Rebecca had marked the bloodstains. Were they getting worse? Should he call her to check? He made his way back to bed first. He didn't want her to know he had taken her suggestion for getting around.

He lay down with a sigh of relief just as he heard her coming up the stairs. She came quietly to his side. After several minutes of silence, he couldn't stand it anymore. "Has the bleeding stopped?"

"It has. I'm sorry if I woke you."

"I wasn't asleep."

"There isn't any way for me to know that unless you speak, Samuel."

"I did speak."

"After I stood here in awkward silence for ages. Are you worn out after your stroll?"

He almost denied that he had been up, but thought better of it. "How did you know?"

"I noticed the papers on your desk had been disturbed and one was on the floor. The window isn't open, so I knew they couldn't have blown around."

"I bumped into it."

"I thought so."

He grudgingly gave her credit for her good idea. "Leaning against the wall makes it easier."

"I'm glad my suggestion was helpful."

He heard the front door open. "Samuel, I'm back. I'm sorry I was gone for so long. How are you?"

His mother came charging up the stairs, breathless by the time she reached his bedside.

"I'm fine, *Mamm*."

"So many people have stopped by to ask about you. I must've told the same story about your injury ten times already today. I thought I would never get free."

"Samuel and I have gotten along fabulously. I changed his sheets. He was up in the chair and even took a short walk. I'm very pleased with him."

His mother laid her hand on his cheek. "You haven't overdone it, have you, Samuel? The doctor warned against that. I would feel dreadful if you suffered a setback. Is the pain worse? I don't know why she thought you needed to be up."

He'd forgotten the pain in his hands and his face for a short time while he was talking with Rebecca. They came roaring back to life now although the pain pill was taking the edge off. "I might have overdone it."

"Is that blood on your bandages?"

"It's nothing to worry about. He bumped it, but the bleeding has stopped," Rebecca said calmly.

"You shouldn't have let him get up."

"Maybe we should let him rest for a while and discuss this downstairs," Rebecca suggested.

"An excellent idea. You and I need to have a talk."

Samuel knew that tone. His mother wasn't happy. He felt a stab of pity for Rebecca, but quickly smothered it. She would be on her way home shortly.

He was glad about that, wasn't he?

Anna Bowman was upset.

Rebecca followed her to the kitchen and prepared to receive a scolding. She didn't have long to wait.

Anna spun to face her with her arms clasped across her chest. "I'm grateful you came to help, Rebecca, but my husband made a mistake in bringing you here. You have overtired Samuel, and I won't have that."

"He is tired, but he can do more than you think. He needs to do more."

"I know how to take care of my own son better than anyone. If you had children, you would realize the truth of that."

Rebecca kept her face carefully blank, but she cringed inwardly. She would never have children of her own unless she married again, and she couldn't see herself with anyone other than Walter. She stiffened her spine, determined not to let Anna drive her away. "Your son isn't a child. He shouldn't be treated like one."

"I know you mean well, but I won't be dictated to by you. Now, I've got to get supper started. The men will be in soon."

Before Rebecca could reply, the outside door opened. Isaac Bowman and his three sons filed in. They all nodded toward her and bid her welcome.

"Smells *goot*!" Noah said with a broad grin. The youngest of the Bowman siblings, Noah was nineteen and still in his *rumspringa*—the years when Amish youth were allowed to sample things normally forbidden to baptized Amish members. He wore blue jeans and a red plaid shirt. His curly brown hair was cut short beneath a black ball cap. He whipped it off at his mother's frown and hung it on the pegs by the door where his father and brothers had placed their identical straw hats.

Anna glanced with surprise at the stove where Rebecca's chicken and noodles were simmering. Apparently she had been so intent on returning to Samuel that she hadn't noticed the enticing smell.

Isaac looked around in satisfaction. "The house looks *wunderbarr*. The floor is spotless. The counters are clean and neat. It's *goot* to have my industrious wife back. I knew bringing Rebecca to look after Samuel was exactly what you needed. You have always kept our home as neat as a pin until Samuel's accident."

Anna glanced around the room. "Well, I try."

Rebecca took pity on the woman. "I wasn't able to get the biscuits started, Anna. Would you like me to do that, or would you like me to sit with Samuel?"

"Well, I don't know." Anna chewed the corner of her lip as she gathered her apron into a wad.

"Let her sit with Samuel," Isaac said. "No one makes biscuits as good as yours."

Anna looked as if she wanted to argue, but instead she nodded. "Tell Samuel that I will be up to feed him as soon as the family is finished with supper."

"Anna, I brought Rebecca here to lighten your load. Let her do her job."

Anna folded her arms over her chest. "She made supper and picked up the house. It was a kindness and I thank her, but I can take care of my own family."

Rebecca caught Isaac's eye. "Samuel asked that Timothy help him this evening."

Isaac arched one eyebrow but didn't comment. Rebecca hoped he understood Samuel's reluctance to be seen as an invalid by others, even by her. She turned to the young men washing up at the sink. "Do you mind, Timothy?"

"I don't mind a bit." Timothy dried his hands on a towel and tossed it over Noah's head. Noah snatched it off and gave his brother a good-natured grin. "You make a fine nursemaid, Timmy. I'm not surprised he asked for you."

"Better to be the nursemaid than the baby." Timothy laughed at Noah's quick scowl and then went upstairs.

Anna smoothed her apron. "May I speak to you privately, Isaac?"

"Of course." He followed her into another room.

Rebecca sighed deeply. She had been too forceful, too pushy, too sure that she knew what was best. She had allowed her experience with her husband's illness to cloud her judgment. Samuel wasn't Walter. Anna would see that she was sent home. It was a shame, because Anna really did need help even if she wouldn't admit it.

"How is he?" Luke asked. He had a wary look about him. Standing apart from the others near the front door, he looked ready to make a quick escape. She had the feeling he was as much an outsider in the home as she was.

Rebecca smiled to put him at ease. "Samuel is healing, but these things take time."

Luke shoved his hands in his pockets. "He's been like a bull with a sore head. Nothing pleases him."

Noah hung his towel on the rod at the end of the

counter. "*Mamm* says we must be patient with him and do everything we can for him."

Luke moved to take his turn at the sink. "That's what we've been doing, and his mood hasn't improved."

"Sometimes doing everything for a person does more harm than good." Rebecca moved to the stove, lifted the lid off the pot and stirred the contents. Fragrant steam rose in a cloud.

"What do you mean?" Noah asked.

She decided the noodles needed a few more minutes and replaced the lid. "Just that if you don't encourage your brother to try harder, he will only grow weaker."

Luke rinsed his hands and turned off the water. "Samuel has never been the weak one."

"That's why this is so hard for him." Rebecca glanced toward the doorway where Anna and Isaac stood. She couldn't tell what decision had been reached, if any.

Isaac hooked his thumbs through his suspenders. "Let's get out of the way until supper is ready. Noah, you owe me a chance to beat you at checkers."

The men left the kitchen. Anna began mixing the biscuit dough. "Rebecca, will you set the table? The dishes are in the cabinet on the left side of the sink."

"Of course." At least she wasn't being sent home before supper. She knew that Isaac was on her side, but how much sway did his wife's wishes hold?

Supper was a quiet meal. After a silent blessing, the food was passed around with a minimum of fuss. Amish meals were not a time for small talk. Isaac laid out the work they would need to do the following day. Other than a few brief questions from his sons, their attention was given to the food. When the meal was over, Isaac took a tray upstairs to Samuel. Timothy offered to do it, but his father brushed aside the offer.

Samuel struggled into a sitting position on the side of his bed when he heard footsteps enter his room. He was feeling more human after Timothy had helped him bathe, and his appetite had been whetted by the wonderful smells from the kitchen. "It's about time."

"If you are impatient for your meal, you should come down to the table."

Tensing at the sound of his father's voice, Samuel quickly apologized. "I'm sorry, Father, I thought you were Timothy. He said he was bringing up my supper."

"I wanted to talk to you, and I thought this was a good time to do it."

"What did you want to talk about?" Samuel heard the sound of the tray being placed on his bedside table and the scrape of the chair legs as his father pulled up a seat beside the bed.

"Your mother is unhappy that I brought Rebecca here."

"I don't blame her. The woman is touched in the head. She actually poured water on my sheets to get me out of bed."

To Samuel's chagrin, his father began chuckling. "I never would've thought of that. Did it work?"

"That is hardly the point."

"Isn't it? Open your mouth. I have a spoonful of chicken and noodles for you."

"Mother said I was to stick with broth."

"Doesn't sound like much of a meal to me. Open."

Samuel did as his father bid. The first bite had his stomach rumbling for more. The noodles were firm, not mushy. The chicken was tender and the chunks of vegetables were done to perfection.

"She's a good cook, I think," his father said, giving him several more bites.

"Not bad, but I'm still glad she isn't staying." Samuel opened his mouth for another spoonful. Although he was embarrassed to be fed by his father, he was hungry enough to accept the help.

After a few more bites, his father spoke again. "How are you feeling, *sohn*? Really. Don't tell me *fine*. I know that isn't true."

"I have a lot of pain. My eyes burn like the fire is still in them. My hands are useless. I hate being helpless."

"I'm sorry God has placed this burden on you. I would take your place if I could."

"I know that. I'm sorry my carelessness placed such a burden on you. I know you need my help in the fields."

"Our neighbors have been lending a hand."

"That's nice to hear. My brothers can't do it all, not without Joshua, but I reckon they'll have to try. It was a bad time for Joshua to marry. They should have waited until the fall like most Amish people do."

"Your brothers are doing fine. Joshua followed his heart and I can't fault him for that. You will be back in the fields in no time."

Samuel's appetite fled. "What if I'm not? What if I'm blind forever as the doctor fears?"

"That is a bridge you can't cross until you reach it. You must have faith that God will provide all you need."

Faith. Did he still possess it?

"Would you like some more supper?" his father asked.

"*Nee*, I'm done."

"Very well. Your mother will be up shortly."

"She's good company." She didn't make him do things he'd rather not.

"She fusses over you."

"I can stand it. She understands that I can't do things for myself."

"All right. *Guten nacht.*"

"Good night." Samuel realized his father hadn't said what he intended to do about Rebecca. "*Daed*, wait."

"What is it, Samuel?"

"You are sending Rebecca home, aren't you?"

Chapter Four

Rebecca had just finished washing the last supper dish when Isaac came downstairs. He handed the bowl and spoon to her before facing his wife. "Samuel would like you to come up now."

Anna turned her back on him and began wiping down the table. "Only if you think I should."

"Of course you should go up. There is no substitute for a mother's love and comfort. Have you any chores that Rebecca can help you with this evening?"

Anna turned around with her arms folded tightly across her chest. "Nothing I can't take care of myself."

"Anna," he chided gently.

"Oh, very well. The gift shop needs dusting. It wouldn't hurt to be swept out, too."

Rebecca washed and rinsed the bowl then dried her hands on a towel. "I will be happy to do that for you. Is there a broom in the building?"

Anna nodded. "There is a broom closet near the back. You'll find what you need in there."

Isaac smiled and nodded at her. She managed a small

smile in return and went upstairs. Rebecca waited for Isaac to speak. Did she have a job or not?

He hooked his thumbs under his suspenders and ran them up and down the bands slowly. "I have spoken with my wife and with Samuel about you staying here."

She laid the towel on the counter. "I assumed you would. They were against it, weren't they? That's okay. The last thing I want is to bring tension into your family."

"Did you really pour water on Samuel to get him out of bed?"

She stared at the towel. "I did, but only a little on his feet. His sheets needed to be laundered, and he refused to get up."

"I would have paid good money to see that."

The laughter lurking in Isaac's voice caused her to jerk her head up. He was grinning. She smiled in relief. "Samuel was quite upset."

"But he got out of bed."

She had to tell the whole truth. "He did, but he fell later when he tried to get back on his own. I don't think he did serious damage to his hands, but I know it hurt him a great deal."

"To try and fail is better than not trying. He and his mother both have trouble asking for help."

"It's a fault many of us share."

"True. I have told them both you are staying. You must be prepared for some resistance."

She drew a deep breath of relief. "*Danki.* I am prepared. Hopefully, I can convince them it's for the best."

"I'm sure you will. My sons need to start cutting corn. They will be in the fields all day tomorrow and I have a table that needs to be delivered to Anna's niece.

I have insisted that Anna come with me. Her niece has a new baby that we have not seen. Samuel has an appointment with his doctor in town. Would you be able to drive him?"

"Of course."

"*Goot.* In spite of what my wife thinks, I believe you will be a great help to this family."

"I hope so. I should go and clean the gift shop before it gets dark. Thank you for keeping me on."

"Anna will show you to your room when she comes back. It is at the back of the house below Samuel's room."

"*Goot.* I should be able to hear if he falls or has trouble at night."

"I wish I could make this easier for you."

She fisted her hands on her hips. "Don't worry about me. I'm a big girl. I can take care of myself."

He chuckled and nodded. "I believe you can."

Rebecca left the house and walked up the lane toward the nearby gift shop with eager steps. She was staying. She didn't have to go home and face her mother's constant pressure to wed John. Her mother meant well, but Rebecca wasn't ready to wed again. She might never be. Her life's mission now was to care for others, for the sick and those in need of help. Her mother refused to accept that.

The sun hung low on the horizon, but she had a good hour of daylight left. Behind the white board fence to her left, the family's horses grazed in the pasture. Six big gray draft horses dwarfed a pair of cream-colored ponies munching beside them while four brown buggy horses stood nose to tail drowsing in the evening air. It was a good farm. A neat farm. The outbuildings and the fences had recently been painted. The animals looked well cared for. The corn in the field across from the horses was tall and turning brown as autumn approached. Orange pumpkins peeked through thick green leaves in a patch behind the gift shop.

She reached the small shop and went in. The door wasn't locked. She hadn't expected it to be. The Amish believed in the goodness of all men and rarely locked their homes or businesses. What did surprise her was that she wasn't alone. Luke was setting up a display of birdhouse gourds just inside the door. He had more in a large box on the floor beside him. They were gaily painted in hues of red, blue and yellow.

She gestured toward them. "Those are pretty. Did you make them?"

"I may not have Samuel's skill with wood, but I'm not without my own talent."

His sour tone shocked her. She folded her hands in front of her. "I never thought otherwise, Luke."

He glanced her way. "You didn't? Aren't you one of those who believe the drugs scrambled my brains?"

"For all I know, your brains were scrambled long before you took drugs. Where is the broom closet?"

A slow smile crept across his face. "You might be the right one to take care of Samuel, after all."

"And why do you say that?"

He rearranged his collection to his satisfaction before turning to her. "You've got a quick wit and a sharp tongue. I don't think you'll take much guff from him."

She saw a door behind the counter and opened it. "I don't imagine he'll give me much guff."

"Oh, he will."

She withdrew a broom and several dusting rags. "Are you worried about him?"

Luke crossed his arms and leaned his hip against the counter to watch her work as she pulled the supplies out of the closet. "Samuel is indestructible."

"No man is indestructible."

"He only cares about what is best for the family. He sees the vine, but he doesn't see the branches. No, I take that back. He sees the branches that need to be pruned away so the vine will prosper."

"Meaning you?" She handed him a dust rag and then began sweeping.

Luke stared at the cloth in his hand for a moment, and then got to work on the shelves filled with jars of apple butter and jams. "Samuel would like it if I left."

"I would be very surprised if that was true."

"You'll see. I've been the thorn in his side since the day I was born."

"Why is that?"

"Because I don't like to do things his way."

"I see. What if his way is the right way? He can't be wrong all the time, can he?"

"Then I do it my way just to annoy him."

She chuckled. "That sounds like my *brudders*. They fight like cats and dogs, but they love each other. Do you think Samuel's accident has changed him?"

"I don't know."

"Your father is worried that it has."

"Maybe Samuel will develop more patience with the rest of us now that he knows what it's like to suffer."

She stopped sweeping and leaned on the broom. "You have suffered, haven't you?"

Luke stopped dusting. "Prison is no picnic. Neither is kicking a drug habit."

"As one who has suffered greatly, do you now have more patience with Samuel?"

Luke gave her a wry smile. "You like to turn people's words back on them, don't you?"

"I like to see all sides of things, even people."

She picked one of his gourds out of the box. "If all I could see was the inside of this house, I might think it was a dark and ugly thing. But I can see the outside is bright and pretty as a flower. Bright outside to delight the eye and attract a nesting pair of birds. Dark inside so the baby birds can sleep. Two sides. Inside, outside. Same birdhouse."

"Samuel is hardly a gourd."

"And neither are you. You are capable of seeing more than one side, too. Samuel is in a very dark place now. He can't see how bright and pretty life is outside of his pain."

She handed the gourd to Luke. "I think you understand how that feels. Samuel is going to need your understanding and your strength to help push him out of his dark nest."

"He won't like it."

"*Nee*, he won't. We'll have to give him a target for his ire."

"You?"

"Why not? I'm not part of the family. I'll leave when he gets well or when he can convince his father to fire me. What do you say? Will you help me help him?"

"Sure. He's going to be mad at me, anyway. He always is."

She resumed sweeping. "*Goot.* What does he like to do?"

"Work. He's always working, and he expects everyone else to work as hard as he does. The woodworking shop was his life. He had high hopes for it. He was sure he could turn it into a prosperous business. Now it's a pile of ashes and twisted metal."

"I heard that members of the church will rebuild it in a few weeks. Once the harvest is done." Rebecca swept the pile of dirt into the dustpan.

"It will be the cost of replacing the machinery that will keep us from reopening anytime soon. And Samuel's injuries. He is a genius with wood. He carves beautiful pieces. It's a God-given gift."

"The Lord gives, and the Lord takes away. We'll have to find a way to include him in the family business even with his limited abilities."

"How?" Luke asked.

She opened the door, tossed out the dirt and then leaned on her broom. "I'm not sure, but the Lord will show us the way if we trust in Him."

Luke looked around the small store. "If Father would consider adding everyday hardware items to this place, we would get more business and Samuel wouldn't have to worry so much about expanding the furniture end of it."

"What kind of things would you add?"

"Battery-operated lanterns. Solar-powered battery chargers. Brooms and mops. Things that won't take up much space, but that people need all the time. Nails, screws, bolts. It's nice to attract the tourists, but the farmers and businessmen in the community have money to spend, too."

"It's an interesting idea. What does your father think of it?"

"I don't know."

"You haven't mentioned it to him?"

"I ran it past Samuel. He said it would be too much work for mother. The gift shop was her idea, and we should leave it alone. Samuel thinks his furniture would bring in more money. He's probably right. Samuel is always right."

"Interesting. You've given me a lot to think about, Luke. I'd also like to buy one of your birdhouses. May I have the red one? You might want to answer your phone."

"What phone?" He tried to look innocent.

"The cell phone set on vibrate in your boot."

His expression fell. "Look, don't tell anyone. Okay?

Rebecca shook her head and walked out the door.

Samuel couldn't believe his own father had turned against him.

He was still fuming the following morning as he lay in bed listening for Rebecca's footsteps. He didn't hear her voice. She wasn't humming or singing today. Where was she? Wasn't she supposed to be making sure he was comfortable? No one had been up to his room since Timothy brought him breakfast. That had been hours ago.

He shifted restlessly on the mattress. Timothy had dressed him in pants and a shirt instead of his pajamas because he had a doctor's appointment in the late morning. It should be almost time to leave. He sat up and swung his feet over the side of the bed. He had his socks on, but he needed his shoes. It was hot, even with his sleeves rolled up past his elbows. He wanted his window opened. Where was that woman? "Rebecca!"

"What is it, Samuel."

He jumped when her soft reply came from nearby. "How long have you been in here?"

"I came up when Timothy was feeding you breakfast this morning."

"You've been standing in my room this whole time?"

"*Nee*, I've been sitting at your desk mending socks and shirts for your mother. What do you need?"

"I need you not to be creeping into my room."

"I didn't creep. I walked."

"Announce yourself next time. I don't like being spied on."

"I can see how it would feel that way. I'm sorry. I was trying not to disturb you per your mother's instructions."

"Sing or hum like you did yesterday so I know where you are."

"Okay. Are you ready to head to the doctor?"

"Who is going to help me get downstairs?"

"I am."

"By yourself? You're not strong enough."

"I'm not going to carry you, Samuel. I'm going to walk down with you and lead you to the buggy."

"What if I fall?"

"You won't. I forbid it. Your shoes are right here. Pick up your left foot."

He lifted his right one.

She sighed. "Luke isn't the only one in this family who seeks to annoy others. You should be ashamed of yourself."

"At least I don't pour water on people in their sick-beds."

She slipped his shoe on and tied the laces. "Didn't I apologize for that?"

"I don't think so."

"Then I'm sorry. Please forgive me."

He held up his other foot. She didn't touch him. After another minute, his patience grew thin. "What are you waiting for?"

"Forgiveness."

"I forgive you."

"Is that true forgiveness?"

"What?"

"You can say you forgive someone without really meaning it. Am I truly forgiven?"

"*Ja*, Rebecca Miller, I have truly forgiven you for pouring water on me as long as you never do it again."

"I'm not sure true forgiveness can be conditional, but it will do. *Danki.* And I have forgiven you, too."

Forgiven him? "For what?"

"For trying to get me fired."

"We both know how that turned out. Can I have my other shoe, please?"

"I have it right here." She slipped it on and tied it. "There, now you are ready. The horse is hitched, and the buggy is waiting outside."

He wasn't ready. The thought of going down the stairs let alone riding in a buggy without being able to see was terrifying.

It shouldn't be. They were things he'd done his entire life. Simple, ordinary things.

Like putting gasoline in the generator. He'd done that a thousand times, too.

"There is an old Amish proverb that says courage is only fear that has said its prayers. I will be with you every step of the way." Rebecca's soft voice sent a flush of embarrassment through him. He didn't want her feeling sorry for him.

"Fine. Let's get it over with." He shot to his feet and wobbled slightly. She grasped his elbow to steady him and steered him toward the door. He struggled not to show his discomfort.

"The stairwell is directly in front of us. I'll go down first, but I'll only be a step below you. Keep your elbow or shoulder against the wall to help maintain your balance. Take it very slowly. If you feel weak or dizzy, just sit down on the step behind you."

"If we wind up in a heap at the bottom, I'm going to say I told you so."

She laughed softly. For some reason it helped steady his nerves. "The first step is right in front of you."

It wasn't as hard as he had imagined, but that didn't make it any less frightening. Thankfully, they reached the bottom of the steps without incident. He took a steadying breath. "Lead on."

"You're doing fine." She had his elbow again.

"I know." He wasn't, but as long as she thought he was, that was good.

"I've got something for you to drink before we get started. It's warm ginger tea. It should be cool enough to sip through a straw. Open."

He pulled his head back. "Why?"

"It will settle your stomach."

"There's nothing wrong with my stomach."

"Please, it will keep you from getting sick on the ride."

"I won't get sick, and I don't want your tea."

"Oh, very well. Here is your hat." She slapped it on his head.

He tried to adjust it, but his bandaged hands were too clumsy. "It's not straight."

She pushed up, pulled down and twisted it back and forth. "Now is it straight?"

"I doubt it, but I reckon it will have to do." He couldn't accomplish the simplest task by himself. Depending on her was galling.

She led the way outside. A fresh breeze was blowing. He could smell the scent of newly cut corn and hear the sounds of the grain binder in the distance. His brothers must be working in the cornfield along the river. He should be there to oversee the work. Luke didn't care how things got done, and Noah spent as much time trying to get out of work as he did working. Timothy could do the job, but he was slow and methodical. "What's the forecast for the next three days?"

"The newspaper said sunny and warm today with a chance of rain in the late afternoon."

"How much of the field do they have cut already?"

"I can't be sure. It looks like about a quarter of it."

"They'd better step it up or they won't get finished before it rains."

"I'm sure they know that. Here is the buggy. Do you want to drive or shall I?"

Did she have to make a joke of everything? "Very funny. You're always laughing at me."

"*Nee*, Samuel. I'm simply trying to lighten your mood."

"There's nothing wrong with my mood."

"From where I'm standing, there is."

"Feel free to go home."

"That's a good idea. I'm sure your father won't mind if I borrow his buggy. Have a nice day, Samuel. The house is behind you. I'm sure you can find your way back."

"You won't leave me here alone without anyone to look after me." Sweat broke out on his brow at the thought.

"Wouldn't I? It wouldn't be any harder than pouring water on your sheets."

She was a heartless woman. "All right."

"All right, what?"

"I believe you. You're just nuts enough to do it. Lead me to the buggy."

"You should stop insulting me. I'm here to help. You should be thanking me for taking you to the doctor."

Samuel pressed his lips tightly together. When she didn't lead him forward, he knew what she was waiting for. He loosened his lips enough to mutter, "I'm grateful for your help, Rebecca."

"There, that wasn't so bad, was it?" Her chipper tone rubbed him the wrong way, but he refrained from commenting. At this rate, they would never reach the doctor's office.

And maybe that wasn't a bad thing. Would the doctor tell him today he would be permanently blind? If he didn't go, he could hold on to the slender hope that he might see again one day. If the doctor told him there was no hope, what would he do? Pray for a miracle? Accept his fate as God's will?

No matter what he was told, he knew the dressing changes would be unbearably painful. He had experienced them three times a day when he was in the hospital and each time was as painful as the last. Knowing he would only have to endure them twice a week was the best part of getting out of the hospital.

"The buggy is in front of you. Raise your foot and feel for the floorboard." Rebecca took his arm. In spite of the way she irritated him, there was something comforting in her touch. Her hands were small and soft. A tingle of awareness lingered on his skin where her fingers gripped him. He tried to ignore the sensation as he climbed in, being careful not to jar his hands. When he was settled, she produced a pillow for him to rest them on.

He felt the dip of the buggy as she climbed in. "Are you okay?"

"Peachy."

She clicked her tongue to get the horse moving. "If you start to feel ill, let me know and I will stop."

"I'll be fine. Just get me there."

The heavy odor of charred wood hung in the air, and he knew they passed the wood shop on their way to the end of the lane. The burned remains of his father's business were one thing he was glad he couldn't see.

If only he hadn't been in such a rush that day. If only he'd taken the time to let the machine cool down. If only he hadn't convinced his father to invest the last of the family's savings in the venture. They were on the brink of ruin and all because of him. When the harvest was done, his brothers would have to look for work elsewhere.

All Samuel had ever wanted in life was to keep the family together. Instead, he would be responsible for sending them away.

Rebecca turned out onto the highway and before long

he could tell they had entered the covered bridge over the river. The sounds of the horse's hooves echoed inside the massive timbered structure that had been built at the turn of the century. It was two lanes wide and spanned the river above the place where his ancestors had run a ferry service that had given the community the name of Bowmans Crossing. A covered pedestrian walkway had been added to the west side of the bridge when he was a child after a car struck and killed two of his classmates on their way to school. It was one of the few covered bridges with a walkway for those on foot, and his father had been instrumental in getting the community to add it.

Someone called a cheerful greeting, and Rebecca answered.

"Who was that?" he asked.

"The bishop's wife. How are you doing?"

"I said I'll be fine. Stop fussing."

"As you wish." Her smug tone made him determined to enjoy the trip.

Within ten minutes, he realized he wasn't going to be fine. The trip to the physician's office would take a little over an hour depending on which horse was in harness. If it was Noah's high-stepping Standardbred mare, they could make the trip in forty minutes. If it was his father's slow and steady horse, it could take well over an hour. To him, it seemed as if they were crawling along. Rebecca was good enough to warn him when the occasional car approached. The sound of them rushing past was less unnerving if he knew they were coming.

The carriage rocked and swayed as they traveled along the highway. Unable to see, he had nothing to distract him as a queasy sensation began to build in his midsection. He started taking deep breaths.

Rebecca pulled the buggy to a stop. "Would you like some of that tea now?"

He nodded. "I think I would."

She produced it in an amazingly short amount of time. He took a sip from the straw she held, and his stomach immediately felt better. He finished the drink. "I should have listened to you."

"Did I just hear you right?" The undercurrent of laughter in her voice drew a smile from him.

"When I'm wrong, I admit it."

"As we all should. I have a few gingersnap cookies if you would like them."

"I think I'll be fine, now. Save them for the trip home. How much longer?"

"A few more miles. Are you up to it? We can wait as long as you need."

"I'm ready.

He heard the slap of the reins against the horse's rump and the buggy jerked forward. He tried to concentrate on anything other than his stomach. "Which horse are you driving?"

"A brown fellow with a white star on his forehead. No one told me his name."

"Father's horse, Gunther. He's not very fast, but he's got stamina."

"Noah offered to let me use his horse, but she looked like a handful."

"She is. My little brother likes the flashy spirited ones."

"Most boys his age do. Is he courting someone?"

"I don't think so. Why?"

"I saw him talking to a young woman this morning out by the road."

"A redhead?"

"She had auburn hair."

"That's just Fannie Erb. She's the daughter of a neighbor. She and Noah have been friends for years. They're both nuts for horses. Her father raises them."

"Is that what Noah wants to do? Raise horses?"

Samuel's queasiness continued to subside. "He wants to drive fast horses and make a fool of himself."

"He strikes me as a serious young fellow."

"Noah? Serious? You've mistaken him for someone else."

"You, perhaps. You're the serious one among the boys."

Was she able to gauge that from her limited contact with him or had she been talking to someone else about him. "I'm the one who sees that things get done."

"There's nothing wrong with that."

"Too bad not everyone feels that way."

"Who feels differently?"

"Luke for one." Samuel normally didn't care to discuss his differences with his brothers, but talking to Rebecca was better than concentrating on his unsettled stomach.

"Luke respects you."

"You're confusing him with someone else now. Luke doesn't respect anyone."

"You're his big brother. He looks up to you. Before you say anything, I can assure you I've seen the way he longs for your approval."

"My approval? You're mistaken."

"I'm not. A word of praise from you would go a long

way in helping Luke deal with his troubles. When a person doesn't feel appreciated or respected by the family, they can lose their sense of belonging and start looking for other ways to fill that void."

Was she right? Maybe he hadn't given Luke enough credit for the difficulties he had overcome.

"Oh, no."

The dismay in her voice caught him by surprise. "What's wrong?"

"Nothing." Her quick reply didn't ring true. Why was she upset? She slowed the buggy and stopped. He heard the sound of another buggy pull alongside.

Chapter Five

"Guder mariye, Rebecca."

Samuel tried to place the jovial man's voice. Who was he?

"Good morning, John." Rebecca's reply was anything but lighthearted. It was more like long-suffering, but at least Samuel realized who the other person was. It was John Miller, her late husband's brother.

"Good day, Samuel Bowman!" John shouted.

Why was he yelling? "*Guder mariye*, John."

"I was sorry to hear about your injury!"

"I'm blind, not deaf, John. I can hear you just fine."

"Oh. Right. How are you?" John's embarrassed tone said he got the point.

"Fine. And you?"

"As right as rain. I'm glad I ran into you, Rebecca. Your mother and I miss seeing you."

"Nonsense. I haven't been gone that long. You can hardly miss someone who has only been gone a day."

Something in Rebecca's voice surprised Samuel. He leaned back slightly. Was she flustered by this chance meeting with her brother-in-law? It sure sounded that way. What did that mean? Had there been bad blood between the brothers? Samuel didn't recall anyone mentioning it. John was a widower. Could it be that he was courting Rebecca? If that was the case, why was she so reluctant to return to her own home? Was it because she truly wanted to help Samuel and his family or was there another reason?

"I don't think there's a restriction on missing someone whose company you enjoy." John sounded disappointed with her response.

"I agree," Samuel added. "I have known my *mamm* to say she sometimes misses my *daed* the moment he walks out the door."

"Your parents have been married a long time," she said with an edge in her tone. She wasn't happy with his interference.

Good. Let her be the one to be annoyed for a change. "I don't think it has to do with time. I think it has to do with how much they enjoy each other's company."

"That's exactly what I was saying. I enjoy your company, Rebecca," John added happily.

"And I'm sure she enjoys your company, John. Don't you, Rebecca?" Samuel said.

"Of course I do. My husband's brother is always welcome in my home. However, I have a job to do, and that job is to get you to your doctor on time, Samuel. Please, excuse us, John. We need to get going."

"Surely a minute or two won't make a difference. Besides, I was to pass on a message from your mother if I saw you."

John was determined to spend a few more minutes in her company. Samuel caught the edge of desperation in his voice and wondered at it.

"And what is the message?" Rebecca asked with reluctance.

Samuel grew more amused by the minute. The woman who had an answer for everything seemed to be struggling today. There was something simmering beneath the surface between John and Rebecca, but he couldn't figure out what it was.

John said, "Your mother wants to know if you are coming home on Sunday. She thought we could all go to the preaching together."

"I can't," Rebecca said quickly.

Too quickly. Samuel smothered a smile. "You don't need to stay with me. I'm sure my family can look after me for one day. You should go home on Sundays."

"Your father and I didn't agree to that." Her terse tone told him to mind his own business, but this was too much fun.

"John, I can assure you that my father will give Rebecca the time off."

"*Goot!* It's settled. I will pick you and your mother up at seven Sunday morning. Good day to you, Samuel. I pray God heals you quickly."

Samuel heard the sound of John's buggy moving away. "Nice fellow."

"*Ja.*" She slapped the reins against the horse and the buggy jolted ahead.

Her clipped tone implied she was done with the subject, but he wasn't. He sensed that John was somehow a raw nerve for Rebecca. He wished he could see her face. Unable to resist needling her, he pressed ahead, "He's been a widower for a while now, hasn't he?"

"*Ja.*"

"A man can get lonely after a time. Maybe he's looking to marry again."

"You would have to ask him about that."

"He was recently chosen to be a minister in the church. He could be a deacon or even a bishop one day."

"I reckon that's true. If God wills it."

"He's a farrier. That's a *goot* job with a steady income. He could support a family easy enough."

"You sound like you've been talking to my mother."

So the subject had come up at home. Samuel chuckled. "It's hard to be on the receiving end, isn't it?"

"I don't know what you mean," she answered primly.

"*Ja*, you do. I'm going to take a stab in the dark here and say that your mother thinks John would make a good husband for you."

"Poke fun all you like. You won't get a rise out of me."

"I'm not looking to get a rise out of you, but meeting John has put me in mind of some work he can do for us. Be sure to tell him that on Sunday. He's welcome to come by any day he is free."

"You don't have work for him."

"But we do. Timothy was saying just the other day that the ponies need new shoes. Noah normally does the shoeing, but we could have John do it since my brothers are all busy. I'll let *Daed* know. *Mamm* might ask John to supper afterward."

"Don't invite him on my account."

"Why not? Do you have something against the man?"

She was silent for so long that Samuel thought he'd pushed his teasing too far. Then she said, "I don't have anything against John. He's a fine man. He was a great help to my husband and me when Walter was sick. John has helped when I needed repairs to the house, and he does little things for my mother. I'm grateful for his kindness."

"But what?" He sensed there was more to her meaning than she was saying.

"But nothing. He's a fine man. We are almost to town. I can't remember if the doctor's office is right or left at the traffic light."

"Left." Samuel decided to let her drop the subject of her brother-in-law, but that didn't keep him from wondering about the relationship between them. He wished he could see her face. He had always considered himself good at reading people. If a man's words were jovial but his smile wasn't reflected in his eyes, Samuel knew the fellow was putting on a front.

He was handicapped in more ways than one when it came to understanding Rebecca. Was it shyness that caused the tension in her voice when she spoke to John? Did she dislike the man for some reason? Or was she playing it cool, hoping her feigned disinterest would capture John's attention?

Samuel had a hard time believing Rebecca could be coy, but no man understood the workings of a woman's mind. Besides, when the heart ruled, good sense often went out the window. He'd seen that often enough with his friends. He intended to avoid the pitfalls of romance himself. The family needed him to manage the woodworking business and expand it. He couldn't be distracted by marriage and a family. Not now. Not until he had the family business up and running again. If he couldn't see or if his hands didn't heal properly, that would never happen. He would become a burden on his family and that was the last thing he wanted.

He had to get better. He would promise God anything if only the Lord would heal him. Imagining a lifetime of darkness sent chills down his spine. He couldn't live that way.

"We're here."

He had been so engrossed in his fear that he hadn't realized the buggy had stopped. Now he was about to face that fear head-on. He dreaded hearing the doctor's words. He dreaded the pain. "Why don't you take me home, instead?"

Rebecca laid her hand on his forearm. "It's going to be okay, Samuel. No matter what troubles come into our lives, our Lord is always with us. With His love in our hearts we can bear all things."

Her gentle touch brought him a sense of comfort and something more. Her voice was soothing and yet stirring. Her palm lay warm against his skin. The scent of lavender enveloped him now that the buggy wasn't moving. A flush of heat traveled up his arms and pooled in his chest, making his heart beat faster.

"You smell nice."

He heard her quick indrawn breath. She pulled her hand away. "I was cutting up sprigs of lavender last evening to make another sachet. Some of them fell into the pocket of my apron. I meant to shake them out and I forgot."

She sounded flustered and a little breathless. The sensation of warmth faded from where she had touched him. He missed it and wanted the comfort of her touch again. He wished he knew what she was thinking.

"We should go in." She got out, and the breeze dispelled the faint fragrance along with the odd fog in his brain.

It wasn't possible that he was attracted to her, was it? *Nee.* Surely not. She was stubborn, willful and brash. She could be kind, but more often than not, she was poking fun at him. He wouldn't be attracted to her. He wasn't.

Besides, he had far more important things to consider.

Rebecca was thankful there wasn't anyone close enough to see her face. She knew by the heat in her cheeks that she was blushing. *You smell nice.* Three simple words were all it took to send her pulse skittering wildly.

Three simple words in his gravelly voice underlined by faint wonder. She shivered again just thinking of it. She would remember to shake out her pockets from now on. She had touched him to offer comfort. Instead, the feeling of his strong muscles and the sight of her pale hand against his dark tanned skin unleashed a surge of emotion she wasn't ready to face.

Samuel required her help. He required her compassionate care. To consider there was anything else between them was unacceptable.

She came around to his side of the buggy. He stepped down without her assistance before she reached him. She took his arm above his elbow making sure she touched only his sleeve and gently guided him into the doctor's office.

After checking Samuel in, Rebecca led him to one of the blue upholstered waiting room chairs that lined the walls. A television was playing in the corner of the room. Three *Englischers* were watching a news channel. Rebecca ignored the distraction and focused on

Samuel. Leaning closer, she spoke softly in Pennsylvania Dutch. "How is your stomach?"

"Better now that I'm not moving. I wish they would get this over with."

"Do you think your father should expand the gift shop to include hardware items?"

"Are you talking about Luke's harebrained scheme?"

"What is harebrained about it?"

"Tourists don't want to see nuts and bolts. They want to see Amish-made jams and jellies, Amish-made cookies and cakes. They want to buy Amish-made furniture and hand-stitched quilts."

"That is true, but having a handy place to buy essentials locally could bring in a fair amount of business. I know John has complained that he has to travel all the way to Berlin when he needs new hoof picks or rasps. A lot of farmers take care of their own horses. You said yourself that Noah normally shoes yours. Where does he get his tools when he needs new ones?"

"The hardware store in Berlin."

"It is something to think about. Luke makes very pretty birdhouses. Did you know that?"

"I knew he carved holes in a few dried gourds."

"Oh, it's much more than that. He has a talent for decorating them. I purchased two. I know several of my *Englisch* friends who would love to have them hanging in their yards and even give them as gifts. I see no reason why Luke couldn't sell dozens of them."

"You think so?"

"I do. It's a shame he doesn't have a way to advertise them."

The nurse came to the waiting room door and called

Samuel's name. Rebecca's heart went out to him when she saw how he tensed. He knew it was going to be painful.

Samuel allowed the nurse to lead him into the exam room. When he was settled on the padded table, she left the room. He braced himself for the coming torment. The last dressing change had been less painful than the ones he endured in the hospital, but it was still excruciating. The minutes ticked by as he sat by himself. Where was everyone? He hated being left alone.

He heard the door open. "How are you doing, Samuel?" Dr. Marksman asked.

"I've been better."

The young doctor had only recently opened a practice in their rural community. Samuel had never been to a doctor until his accident.

"I'm sure you have been better. How is the pain? Are you getting any sleep?"

"The pain is less, but I don't sleep much."

"All right, let's take a look." He felt the doctor begin to unwrap the bandages over his eyes. He had been told not to expect too much, but he prayed he would see a glimmer of light, if nothing else.

When the last wrap fell away, the doctor removed the pads covering Samuel's eyes. "Open your eyes slowly. I'll dim the lights if it is too bright in here for you."

Samuel let his lids flutter briefly, then opened his eyes fully. The room was pitch-dark. "I can't see anything. Turn up the lights."

He felt the doctor's fingers under his chin. He turned Samuel's face in one direction and back again. "The inflammation I first observed is better. The lights are on, Samuel."

"Then why can't I see?" Samuel's heart began hammering in his chest. His palms grew sweaty.

"Let me try something." The doctor stepped away and came back a few seconds later. "What about now?"

"Nothing. I'm still blind. Why can't I see?"

Still blind.

Blind for life. Forever.

The words tumbled over and over in Samuel's mind. He had trouble listening to the doctor. Dizziness made his head swim. He couldn't catch his breath.

Dr. Marksman laid a soothing hand on Samuel's shoulder. "It's going to take a little more time, that's all. I would still like you to see a specialist."

Samuel forced himself to slow his breathing. He shoved the fear to the back of his mind. This was what God had planned for him. He would accept it. "We can't afford to see a specialist. What would he do for me that you aren't doing?"

"That's a valid question. I'm treating your burns and letting your eyes rest and recover on their own, but I'm not familiar with this type of eye injury. A specialist might have other ideas about treatment. At least let me consult with one."

"There is no harm in that if it doesn't cost me anything."

The doctor applied ointment to Samuel's eyes and covered his face with new bandages. "Are your parents with you today?"

"*Nee*, my father is harvesting corn. Rebecca Miller brought me."

"Ah, I know Rebecca. She would have made an excellent nurse if she hadn't chosen the Amish way of life. She knows how to follow instructions and what to look for."

Samuel heard the door open. The doctor spoke to someone in the hallway outside. "Nurse, will you have Rebecca Miller step in, please."

Great. "Does she have to be in here?"

"No, but I definitely need to know someone understands how to take care of you. You aren't in a position to see what's going on. Will you allow me to discuss your condition with her present?"

"I reckon."

"Nurse, bring an information consent form, too. You and I will have to sign it as verbal witnesses to Mr. Bowman's wishes."

"Yes, Doctor."

A few minutes later, the door opened. Samuel caught a whiff of lavender and knew Rebecca had come in.

"Hello, Dr. Marksman. It's good to see you again."

"You, too, Rebecca. Mrs. Stulzman and her new baby are getting along fine. I thought you'd want to know."

"How nice."

"Samuel, you are blessed to have this woman looking after you."

He pressed his lips closed. Rebecca laughed softly. "I'm afraid Samuel doesn't see me as a blessing."

"Well, he should. I want you to take a close look at his injuries. You should put on a pair of gloves when changing his bandages just to keep things clean." The doctor began unwrapping Samuel's left hand.

When the air hit his tender skin, Samuel sucked in

a sharp breath. Rebecca did the same. "That looks so painful."

"It is," Samuel said through gritted teeth.

The doctor removed the last of the dressings. "Samuel had mostly second-degree burns, but some of them are very deep and may be third-degree. The blisters that are broken are second-degree burns for sure. Those that continue to fill and ooze are most likely third-degree. They will produce some scarring. The burn can go one of two ways. The blisters will dry up or break, then the outer layer of damaged skin will also dry and peel off. At this stage, a new outer layer of skin develops. Peeling usually starts several days after the blisters pop. Normally, it takes three to five days for the peeling to run its course. The sensation should shift from pain to itching within a few days after the blisters break, but it can take longer."

That was good news. Samuel was ready for something other than pain.

"The new skin will be very sensitive so even a mild bump will still cause discomfort."

"What are the signs of infection?" she asked.

"If the burn gets infected, the blisters won't dry up. Instead, they'll develop crusty, yellowish scabs that continue to cause pain. If that happens, the crust needs to be softened and removed by applying a washcloth soaked in warm soapy water. Just let it rest on the site until the stuff is soft enough to come away easily. Don't scrub. After the extremity dries, apply an antibiotic cream and cover with a nonstick gauze. If an infection is present and doesn't show signs of improvement within two or three days of using an antibiotic cream, get back here. I'll have to put him on a stronger oral antibiotic."

"I understand."

"I'll show you how to redress these. Make sure his fingers are well separated. We don't want them sticking together."

When they finished both hands twenty minutes later, Rebecca could see the ordeal had taken its toll on Samuel. His lips were pressed into a thin line with a pale ring around them. She took his arm as he stood and noticed he swayed slightly on his feet.

The young doctor handed Rebecca a slip of paper. "I want to see him again in a week. This is a prescription for more pain medication. Make sure he takes it before he comes in next time."

Rebecca frowned at Samuel. "Was he supposed to take some today?"

"Yes. The dressing changes can be very painful. You are doing well, Mr. Bowman. Make sure you drink plenty of liquids and get plenty of rest. Come in sooner if you experience a fever or signs of infection."

"What about his vision?" Rebecca asked.

"It's too soon to tell," Samuel muttered.

The doctor sighed. "I still feel that Mr. Bowman should see an eye specialist."

Samuel shook his head. "It's too far to travel, and it's too expensive. If God wishes my sight restored, it will be so."

"I respect your beliefs, Mr. Bowman, and I pray for your healing." Dr. Marksman smiled sadly at Rebecca and left the room.

"Get me home," Samuel said through gritted teeth.

Rebecca led him out to the buggy and got him settled. "You rest here. I'm going to have this prescription filled. It should only take a few minutes. The pharmacy is right next door."

"Rebecca, I don't need pain pills," he snapped.

"I may need them if you're going to bite my head off all the way home."

"Suit yourself. You always do what you want, anyway. You have no *demut*."

"You're right." It was useless to point out that he was lacking in humility, as well. He was clearly in pain and determined to endure it. Without another word, she walked away and left him to stew while she had his prescription filled. For the next ten minutes, she kept an eye on him through the drugstore window. When she had his medication in hand, she returned to the buggy.

Sitting on the seat beside him, she withdrew a jar of ginger tea from her bag. "I can't bear to see you in such misery, Samuel. Please take one of your pills and some tea. It will help. You do yourself no favor by suffering needlessly."

"All right. Anything. Just take me home."

Relief let her draw a deep breath. *"Danki."*

She gave him the medicine and when he was ready, she backed away from the hitching rail and headed the horse toward Bowmans Crossing.

Samuel was resting in bed when Luke came in with his supper later that evening. "Would you like something to eat?"

"I am a little hungry." Samuel sat up on the edge of the bed.

Luke pulled a small table over and sat in the chair beside him. "Are you in a lot of pain?"

"Some. It's better than it was earlier today. As much

as I dislike Rebecca bossing me around, she was right about the pain medicine. She's not in here, is she?"

"It's just you and me."

"*Goot.* She has a way of sneaking in that's unnerving." And yet he missed her when she wasn't around. She had avoided him all afternoon, leaving his mother to sit with him after they returned. He could hardly blame her. He hadn't been good company. At least the pain meds allowed him to nap briefly. He would have a hard time sleeping later.

"I like her." Luke fed him a bite of mashed potatoes and meat loaf.

Samuel swallowed his mouthful. "You would. She's not a normal Amish woman."

Luke chuckled. "That's for sure. She speaks her mind."

"It's strange, but I can't recall exactly what she looks like. I guess I never paid much attention to her before."

"No reason why you should. She was another man's wife. Our families weren't close. She and her husband lived almost ten miles from here. I don't know about you, but I'm always checking out the single girls, not the married ones."

Samuel ate in silence for the rest of the meal. When he was finished, Luke asked, "Would you like some coffee? I have some right here."

"Maybe half a cup. Is she pretty?"

Luke held the mug to Samuel's lips. "Is who pretty?"

"Rebecca. Who else have we been talking about?"

"Pretty enough, I guess. She has a trim figure, good teeth—she seems strong enough."

"You sound like you are describing a horse."

"Okay, her eyes are a deep violet-blue. Very pretty. She has a direct stare that proves she is listening to you.

Her hair is blond. She's very fair skinned. Her eyes sparkle when she smiles, and she smiles a lot."

"Even when she is browbeating me?"

Luke chuckled. "I think you can take it."

Samuel frowned. It almost sounded as if Luke was becoming infatuated with Rebecca. Was he?

Chapter Six

The idea that his brother might be falling for Rebecca didn't sit well with Samuel, but he wasn't sure why. "She tells me you have made some birdhouses out of the gourds from *Mamm's* garden."

"I've made a few. Rebecca liked them." Luke's tone turned cool.

"She thinks they'll sell well if we can find a way to advertise them. Any ideas?" Was he really going to give credence to her notion?

Even when she wasn't in the room, Rebecca was a hard woman to ignore. The things she said stuck in Samuel's mind as if she had nailed them there. For the past hour, he had been thinking about the sound of her voice and mulling over her praise of Luke's work. Was there something between the two of them? He shifted uncomfortably on the bed.

Samuel heard Luke walk away from the bed. "I haven't thought about ways to advertise. I guess I just hoped someone who stopped in for something else would buy one of my gourds."

"I've been doing some thinking. There's not much

else to do up here. You know that big tree on the north side of the road at the stop sign."

"Sure."

"If you were to hang a few of your birdhouses on that tree within easy reach for folks, you could bolt an honor payment box to the tree and sell them that way."

"That's not a bad idea, Samuel. I could even put out unpainted gourds for folks who would like to decorate their own."

"You could."

"We could add an arrow that points the way to our store in case folks wanted more Amish crafts."

Samuel listened in amazement to Luke's growing eagerness. "What do you think a fair price would be?"

The two men discussed costs and settled on a figure for painted and plain gourds. Samuel remembered Rebecca's comments that Luke needed and wanted his approval. He wasn't used to praising his brothers. It felt odd, but maybe she was right.

"Luke, I appreciate how much you have stepped up to help the family. I know you, Timothy and Noah are shouldering my share of the work along with your own."

"You would do the same. I don't know why you're surprised that I would," Luke said with a hint of resentment.

So much for Rebecca's idea. Even when Samuel tried to be nice, Luke's bad attitude reared its head.

Swallowing his resentment, Samuel tried again. "I'm not surprised that you stepped up. I just wanted to say I appreciate it and I know the rest of the family does, too. The birdhouses are a good idea. Rebecca seems to think they'll make money for us. We're going to need more ideas like it if I—if I can't carve again."

"You will."

"With hands that don't work and eyes that can't see. I'm more likely to become a burden on this family." The anger and sadness in his heart pulled him toward a dark place.

Luke was silent for so long that Samuel wondered if he had left the room. He leveraged himself back into bed. He just wanted to sleep. To forget everything that had happened.

Luke cleared his throat, proving he was still beside the bed. "I never did tell you how sorry I was that I didn't take care of the generator that morning. I should have put gas in it when you told me and not handed the chore off to Noah. I'm so, so sorry." The pain and sorrow in his voice were unmistakable.

Samuel's throat constricted as tears burned behind his bandages. "I don't blame you, Luke. We've disagreed on a number of things over the years, but I never once thought you wanted to hurt me. God chose this path for my feet to walk."

"I wish it had been me." He barely whispered the words as Samuel felt the weight of Luke's hand on his shoulder.

"I don't, *brudder*. Not even for a minute."

Rebecca was seated at the table when Luke came downstairs. She caught a glimpse of him wiping his eyes before he came into the room. She rose to take the tray and dishes from him. "How is Samuel feeling?"

"He's still in pain."

All the dishes on the tray were empty. "At least his appetite is improving."

Luke followed her as she carried the dishes to the sink. "I want to thank you."

She glanced at him over her shoulder. "For what?"

"For telling him about my birdhouses. We've come up with a way to advertise and sell them along the highway."

She smiled at him. "I'm glad."

"He doesn't blame me. I thought he did. I thought he believed it was my fault."

She turned around. "Why would you think that?"

"Because it *was* my fault. I was the one who didn't fill the gas tank that morning. I told Noah to do it, but he was walking away from me and never even heard me. I should have made sure that he was listening. No, I should have done it myself."

"We can't change one minute of the past, Luke. Regrets are useless. We can only change how we move forward."

"I guess you're right. That might take a little practice on my part."

"I have news for you. It isn't easy for anyone."

"What isn't easy?" Noah came in from the living room. He pulled open the refrigerator door and studied the contents.

Luke ruffled his younger brother's hair. "It's not easy keeping you fed."

Noah swatted his hand away and made a muscle with his arm. "I have to keep up my strength. We have more corn to stack tomorrow."

Rebecca dried her hands, opened the cupboard and pulled out a chocolate bundt cake. "I made this earlier."

"Perfect." Noah took the plate from her hands.

Luke snatched it away from him and held it behind

his back. "You can have a piece, but you have to take one up to Samuel. You know how much he likes chocolate cake."

"Did I hear chocolate cake?" Timothy strolled in with a book in his hand.

Rebecca took the plate away from Luke. "Before the three of you inhale it, you should see if your parents want some."

Timothy opened a drawer, pulled out some forks and handed them around. "*Mamm* and *Daed* have gone to bed."

"All the more for us." Noah grabbed a plate drying in the rack on the counter. Luke and Timothy did the same.

"All right." She cut the cake into generous slices and filled each plate the men pressed at her. When Luke held out a second plate, she smiled to herself. "Do I have to supervise or will you actually take it up to Samuel?"

Luke flushed. "We'll all take it up."

"That's a fine idea," Noah declared.

The men trooped up the stairs together. After a few minutes, the sound of quiet laughter drifted down. Smiling, she turned around to see Anna glaring at her.

Rebecca pasted a smile on her face. "Good evening, Anna. I'm sorry if we woke you. The boys wanted some cake."

"You have made yourself right at home with my family."

Rebecca couldn't tell if Anna was upset or not. "Your family has made it easy to feel welcome. You have been blessed in your children. Would you like a piece of cake?"

"I think I would." Anna went to the cupboard and

got her own plate down. She held it out as Rebecca placed a slice on it.

Anna carried her plate to the table and sat down. "Won't you join me?"

Was this an olive branch? "I was about to make some chamomile tea. Would you like some, too?"

"That sounds nice."

Rebecca fixed two cups of tea, cut a small piece of cake for herself and carried it all to the table. She sat down across from Anna and decided to let the older woman lead the conversation. They ate in silence for a few minutes.

"Tomorrow I must go and help my sister-in-law get ready for church services at her home. Edna always waits until the last minute to clean."

"What can I do to help?"

"If you could make the men a light lunch and take it out to the fields tomorrow that would be a blessing."

"Consider it done."

"My husband was right," Anna said without looking up from her plate.

"About what?" Rebecca didn't want to assume anything.

Anna glanced up. "He was right that I needed an extra pair of hands to help with Samuel."

"If I have lightened your burden in any way, then I'm happy I came."

"Samuel spoke about you a lot this afternoon."

"Did he? It wasn't all good, I'm sure."

"He said he noticed John Miller seems quite taken with you."

Rebecca's cheeks flamed red. How did she explain?

"My brother-in-law has been very kind to me since Walter died."

"You don't think it's more than that?"

"Perhaps it is. Our families have been pushing for a match between us."

"It's understandable. John is a widower. There are far more bachelors in Bowmans Crossing than there are single women. You inherited your husband's lands. I'm sure his parents would like to see that land come back to the family."

"I have heard all the arguments about why it would be a beneficial match."

"But?"

"I'm not in love with John. I'm not sure I will ever love anyone the way I loved Walter."

"A good marriage is not always about wide-eyed, heart-thumping love. It should be about respect and common goals. It should be about raising children and teaching them to fear the Lord. Isaac is my second husband. Did you know that?"

Rebecca looked at Anna in surprise "I didn't."

"I came from a small town in Pennsylvania. I had married my childhood sweetheart but he died in a hunting accident a few months later. I didn't believe I could ever love again."

Rebecca understood that sorrow. "I'm sorry for your loss."

"*Danki.* I met Isaac at my cousin's wedding. We courted briefly. When he asked me to marry him, I wasn't in love with him the way I had loved my husband, but I wanted a family and a home of my own, so I said yes."

Rebecca crossed her arms on the table and leaned

toward Anna. "Was it the right decision? Would you do it again?"

Anna stirred her tea slowly. "It was the right decision for me. Over the years, I have come to care deeply for Isaac. He has given me five strong sons and provided for us all. I could not ask for more."

"But, do you love him?"

Anna smiled softly. "There are all kinds of love, child. The love a mother has for her children. The love a man has for his wife. The love God has for all of us. All different, but all love nonetheless. *Ja*, I love him."

Leaning back, Rebecca pushed the last bite of cake around on her plate. Maybe she was wrong to reject John's advances. Maybe mutual respect and common goals would be enough. Maybe.

"Samuel, what are you doing?"

He stopped pacing at the sound of Rebecca's tired, irritated voice. "I'm sorry if I woke you."

"What's wrong?"

Having her near lessened his pain. "Nothing. Go back to bed."

"Something is wrong. Let me help."

Too tired to fight alone, he sighed. "I can't sleep. My hands hurt. My face hurts. The dressing changes always do this."

"I'll get you a pain pill."

"*Nee*. They make me so groggy." He turned and took the five steps he knew would bring him to the open window. The breeze was slight, but it carried a hint of coolness and the smell of the river. He braced his forearms on the window jamb and leaned forward until his forehead rested on the cool glass.

"It's two-thirty in the morning, Samuel. Groggy would not be a bad thing about now." The hint of humor in her voice made him smile.

"They make me hot, and it's already too warm to sleep. I just need to take my mind off of it. I wish I could go outside where it's cool."

"I agree that it's a warm night."

"Really, I'm fine. Go back to bed. I'll stop pacing."

"I'm not sure I can get back to sleep. I'll take you out on the porch for a while."

"I'd rather go down to the river."

"In the dark?" Her voice rose in surprise.

"It's always dark for me. Go back to bed." He tried to keep the bitterness out of his tone and failed.

He heard her bare feet padding across the wooden floor. He wasn't surprised when she laid a hand on his arm. "I'm sorry."

"Don't be. I'll have to get used to comments like that."

"You don't know what God has planned for you. I will take you outside if that is what you want."

"It is. *Danki.*"

She had a long robe on over her nightgown, but she should have put on her shoes.

The grass was cool and damp, but Rebecca discovered a number of small stones with her bare feet as she led Samuel out the back door and toward the water. She used a small flashlight to help her pick a path. The farmhouse was situated on a small knoll that overlooked the river below. The lawn had a gentle slope to it. She was happy to see Samuel had no trouble keeping his balance as they walked slowly along.

"What are the stars like tonight?"

She paused and looked up. "They are hidden behind the clouds. I see only a few peeking through."

"Is the moon up? It should be full tonight."

She studied the heavens and detected a spot of unusual brightness behind the layer of clouds to the east. "It is, but it's behind the clouds. Did you have someplace in mind to go?"

"There is a low stone wall below the bridge. I like to sit there."

She swung her light in that direction. "I see it."

Keeping a firm grip on his elbow, she led him forward until they reached the wall. He sat down with a contented sigh. A fresh breezed rustled the leaves of the trees and shrubs along the bank. The water made faint gurgling sounds as it flowed around the bridge piling. A bullfrog croaked nearby. She turned the light in that direction. She didn't see him, but a loud splash proved he had been hiding in the reeds.

"I love to sit and listen to the river at night."

"Do you?" She swung the flashlight in a wide arc when a rustling in the nearby bushes startled her. A pair of eyes blinked once and vanished. She had no idea who or what they belonged to. Slipping closer to Samuel, she kept her light trained on the shrubbery, but nothing else appeared.

"Being blind isn't so bad at night. I can smell the scent of mud and decay. I can hear the water tug at the branches of the plants lining the edge of the waterway. I know exactly how the river looks when the moon rises and casts its sparkling light on the ripples. It's peaceful, don't you think?"

She jerked the light toward the bridge when she heard the sudden flap of wings. "What's that?"

"An owl who lives in the rafters of the covered bridge. He's going out to hunt. It's so much better out here than being cooped up inside. Don't you agree?"

"It's nice." As long as the eyes didn't show up again and the owl didn't swoop in her direction. It wasn't long before the bugs found her light and began to flutter in front of her. She batted them away and finally snapped it off.

"Close your eyes."

"They are closed." She blinked then checked the bushes again. Nothing showed itself. She didn't like the dark.

"Tell me what you hear?"

"Insects and frogs."

He raised his face to the sky. "I hear the earth slumbering."

Samuel had a fanciful side? She never would have guessed that. "What a beautiful thing to say."

He lowered his face. "It's silly, I know."

"I don't think it's silly at all. God created many wonders. Some we see in the light of day, some are only revealed at night. Have you always liked the night, or is this because of your injury?"

"I've always loved to sit out here after the household is asleep. I like the night sounds. The wind is softer. The air is cooler. The trees sway and dip. Small animals rustle through the leaves and underbrush. Bats and owls glide by with barely a sound."

"Bats?" Something buzzed by her ear, and she swatted at it. What other sort of creepy-crawlies were out here? She scooted a hair closer to Samuel.

"Are you afraid of bats?"

She heard another sound and switched on the light again. "Of course not. What kinds of animals crawl through the leaves?"

"Rebecca Miller, are you afraid of the dark?"

The humor in his tone made her spine stiffen. "Why would you think that?"

"I keep hearing the flashlight click on and off."

"So?" She shut it off and put it in the pocket of her robe.

"We aren't walking. You don't need to see your way, so why are you swinging it around unless it is to make sure something isn't sneaking up on us. Leave the light off, and your eyes will adjust to the darkness."

"It's off, okay?" She slipped another inch closer to him. Without the light, she heard even more sounds.

He chuckled.

"What's so funny, Samuel?"

"If you move any closer, you'll be sitting in my lap. Do you really think a blind man could protect you?"

She wiggled a few inches away. "Maybe. Maybe not. But I could push you down and let the bear eat you while I run away."

"There are no bears around here."

"There are wild dogs. Coyotes. Other things."

"What other things?" She could tell he was struggling to contain his mirth, but she didn't care if he did think it was funny.

"When I was little, my brothers used to tell me that the coyotes and foxes would eat me if I went out of the house at night."

"And you believed them?"

"Maybe." She'd never heard of anyone being attacked, so she was pretty sure they had only said it to frighten her. It worked.

"A coyote is much more afraid of you than you are of him."

"Don't be too sure about that." She closed her hand over the solid cylinder of the flashlight in her pocket. It would make a decent club if need be.

A loud splash made her jump back into Samuel. His arms went around her. She struggled to pull the light out, but Samuel blocked her arm with his elbow. "Wait. You'll see what it is in a minute," he whispered in her ear. His breath sent a shiver across her skin. She was pressed against the length of him. His chest rose and fell with each breath. Her fear of the night faded rapidly.

"That was something big jumping in the water." She used the same low whisper although she wasn't sure why.

"I know."

She strained her eyes, staring at the inky blackness below the bridge. Finally, she made out a shape crossing the river. The clouds broke apart, and the light of the moon silhouetted a huge buck swimming across the river. The moonlight sparkled like diamonds on the V-shaped ripples behind him and the droplets of water on his antlers.

"It's a deer," she whispered, awestruck by the beauty of the scene.

"I thought so. They often cross near here."

"Why don't they use the bridge?"

He laughed. The buck changed course and began swimming downstream until it was out of sight behind some bushes. "They don't use the bridge because they are wild things. To them, it must look safer to swim the river rather than chance entering a man-made cave if they think about it at all."

"I suppose." She stepped away from him and missed the warmth of his contact.

"Are you ready to go?" he asked softly.

Rebecca glanced at the man beside her. He wasn't the invalid she had first come to know. There was much more to Samuel Bowman than met the eye, and she liked what she was learning about him. "Not yet. Are you?"

"*Nee*. I could sit out here for hours. Maybe that's why God took my sight, because I have always liked the night."

"His ways are hard to comprehend."

"I never wanted anything except to take care of this family. Instead, I've become a burden to them. I have lost my father's entire savings along with his business."

"The building can be replaced. Our church will help."

"With the building, but what about the machinery? It will take years of scrimping for my family to replace it. My brothers will have to move away to get jobs when the harvest is over instead of working here. My mother will be heartbroken to lose them. I dread to think how she will feel if Joshua and his new wife can't settle here and raise their children within her sight."

"No one sees you as a burden, Samuel. Your family loves you."

"I don't doubt that now, but what about in the future? What about when they see all that my foolishness has taken away. My save-the-family scheme was a failure. I dread the reproach in their eyes more than I dread the pity I know they have for me now."

She laid a hand on his shoulder. "It will all turn out as He wills. God takes care of our future. We must live for today and leave the rest up to Him."

The simple feel of her hand and her softly spoken words gave him more hope than he'd found in days. What she said was true, but he knew he had to do more. "A man must trust God to give him a good harvest, but he still has to hoe the weeds from the garden."

"Is that what you did out here at night before the accident, hoe weeds?" She pulled her hand away and he missed the comfort of her touch.

"Mostly, I gave thanks out here. It's a fitting place to seek the Lord's guidance and listen to His wisdom."

"You surprise me, Samuel Bowman."

"Why? You don't think of me as a spiritual man?"

"It isn't that. I guess I thought you were the kind of man who gives the Lord thanks at the table and at church services and then doesn't think about Him the rest of the time."

"I reckon I deserve that opinion. I haven't been the best patient."

"You have been stubborn and bullheaded, but you haven't been a bad patient. I once took care of an elderly woman who spit at me every chance she got. I became very quick on my feet."

"I must say you have surprised me, too."

"Because you found out I'm scared of the dark? It is creepy out here, but at least the moon is out now and I can see my hand in front of my face. But who knows what is watching us from the shadows."

"It's surprising that you are afraid of anything. You seem so sure of yourself."

"I have a reason for my discomfort in the dark. Some people thought it was funny to frighten me."

"Your brothers?"

"They started it, but it was my husband who took it up a notch. He would hide and then jump out and scare me when I least expected it. I used to get so mad at him for that."

Her voice, tinged with sad yearning, made Samuel long to comfort her. "You miss him, don't you?"

"Of course I do. It's only natural. But I know he is with God in Heaven."

"What do you miss about him the most?"

"The most? So many things. I think I miss the sound of his voice the most. We would lie awake until all hours of the night just talking about our dreams and our plans. About what went right that day and about what was wrong. I miss him scolding me and telling me to hurry or we would be late to church. We never were. After every meal I made he'd pat his stomach and tell me it was real fine cooking. And jokes! That man was forever telling me jokes. Silly ones, knee-slappers. He loved a good joke."

"Will you marry again?"

She was silent a long time. Had he gone too far? Her personal life was a private matter. He had no business prying into it.

Chapter Seven

Rebecca wasn't sure how to answer Samuel's question. Would she marry again? It seemed that everyone had an opinion about whether she should or not, but how did she truly feel about it?

He waited patiently for her answer. Somehow, it was easier to express her feelings under the cover of darkness. She didn't have to school her features into blankness and pretend that she was content with the way life was. It was easy to confide in Samuel. Maybe it was because he couldn't see her face.

"I don't believe I will marry. I find great satisfaction caring for the sick among us. I can be useful, and I like that."

"A wife and mother does the same. There are many good men in our community."

"I find it hard to imagine someone who could make me laugh the way Walter did. It's harder still to imagine going through life with someone who doesn't make me laugh. I don't think I could abide that."

"That's understandable."

"Is it?"

"You've played some good pranks yourself."

She giggled. "I'm a bully. Say it like it is."

"Okay, I agree with that. Anyone who would pour a glass of water on a blind man."

"Sprinkled, not poured. I sprinkled water on your feet. Give me any more grief about it, and I'll leave you alone out here."

"If I had one good hand I'd take your flashlight away and leave *you* alone out here. I think it would bother you more than it would me. Don't forget, these bandages will come off one day. I may yet have my revenge for that *sprinkle*."

She enjoyed his teasing. Maybe too much. This Samuel was easy to like. "I've been warned. Are you ready to go back to the house?"

"I think so." He stood. "Wait! Do you hear that?"

"You can't trick me so easily."

"Something is coming this way."

Laughing, she jumped to her feet. "I have been assured there are no bears around here, so you can't frighten me."

He held up one hand and tipped his head to the side. "Hush a minute."

He sounded so serious. She bit her lip as she glanced at the bushes nearby. Was it the wind making them move or something else? "Do you really hear something?"

"I do." He turned his head slightly as if trying to locate the sound.

"What is it?" She fumbled for her light and snapped it on as she took a step closer to him.

"I hear…Rebecca Miller quaking in her boots." He sat down and started laughing.

"That is just mean." She punched his shoulder.

"Ouch. I'm an injured man. You can't hit me."

"You should be thankful I don't have a glass of water handy."

Chuckling, he rose to his feet. "I think I can sleep now."

Rebecca's smile faded as she took his arm and led him toward the house. He was doing better, growing more confident, and she was glad. Soon, he wouldn't need her anymore.

With sudden clarity, she realized that she needed to be needed. Without someone to care for, she had been little more than an empty shell waiting for life to be over. She didn't want to go back to that. She wanted to love life again.

Timothy drove her home Saturday evening, and on Sunday morning, as promised, John arrived in his buggy to take her and her mother to church. Rebecca wore her best dark maroon dress with its matching cape and apron. She tied her black traveling bonnet over her *kapp* and pulled on a cloak. Picking up a basket filled with food for the noon meal, she mentally braced herself before joining John and her mother in the buggy.

"Guder mariye," John called out.

"Good morning, John. Good morning, *Mamm.*" Rebecca opened the door to the backseat and deposited her basket on the floor beside her mother's identical one.

John smiled at her as he got down. She had no choice but to climb in beside her mother. John got back in. It was a tight squeeze with all three of them in the front. She was pressed shoulder to hip against him. "It's a fine morning for a buggy ride," he said.

His voice sounded strained although his smile was bright. Too bright. As if he were forcing it.

"Any day we gather to praise God is a fine day," her mother added cheerfully when Rebecca didn't respond.

She didn't doubt they had been talking about her on the way over. Although it wasn't a comfortable trip for Rebecca, it was a pretty one. The hillsides and fields had exploded with fall colors in the past week. The air was crisp but not cold. Her mother kept up a steady flow of chatter that only required an occasional comment. John remained silent as his horse trotted along at a steady pace, and they soon reached the covered bridge over the river.

The weathered red wooden structure blended into the red-and-gold autumn leaves on the trees that grew along the roadway. Wide enough for two lanes of traffic, the opening loomed like a cave. As the horse entered the dark interior, Rebecca stared through the slatted sides at the Bowman house on the hillside across the river. She could see all of them standing in the front yard. It was easy to pick Samuel out among the men wearing identical dark suits and black felt hats. His white bandages stood out in stark contrast to the somber colors.

She lost sight of the family when John's buggy came out the other side of the bridge. A quarter mile farther along, they reached the stop sign on the main road between Berlin and Winesburg.

Rebecca's mother leaned to see around her. "Look at all the birdhouse gourds. Aren't they pretty."

Smiling, Rebecca murmured her agreement. "Very pretty."

A car had pulled off the road and was stopped beneath the spreading branches of the old oak tree. An

Englisch family was looking at the gourds. As John sent his horse across the highway, Rebecca saw the woman select two yellow ones while the man with her placed money in the box Luke had nailed to the tree.

John noticed her looking back. "I wonder who is selling them?"

"Luke Bowman makes them." Rebecca faced forward again.

"You know I did notice a few of them in Anna's shop. It's a very clever idea to display them that way," her mother said.

"Samuel thought of it."

John glanced at her. "I haven't asked. How is the poor man doing?"

"He's getting better every day."

Her mother's eyes filled with sympathy. "Burns can be so painful. Is he suffering a great deal?"

"When the doctor changes his bandages he endures a lot of pain, but he doesn't complain."

John shook his head. "It's a shame his work was destroyed in the fire. I know the family had high hopes for his business."

"Anna told me they had a furniture buyer coming from Cincinnati just to look at Samuel's work. Of course, they had to tell him not to come because of the fire. Samuel made my china cabinet. It's a beautiful piece. Your father bought it for me the year before he died," her mother said.

"I know you cherish it."

John slowed his horse behind several buggies ahead of him. At the front of the line, Rebecca saw an elderly Amish couple moving at a sedate pace along the road. No one passed them. It would be impolite and pretentious to do so on a Sunday. No one wanted to show such a lack of humility on the Lord's Day.

A buggy drew in behind them. Rebecca glanced back and saw the Bowman family had caught up with them. Noah leaned out the side window and waved. His mother spoke sharply to him, and he pulled his head in. Rebecca ducked her head to keep from laughing.

They all arrived together at the home of Roy Bowman a little before eight. Roy was Isaac's eldest brother. Each family in Rebecca's congregation hosted services in their home at least once a year. Since the prayer meetings were held every other Sunday, a family rarely had to host it twice. The long gray bench wagon sat beside the house. Men were unloading the benches that traveled to the designated houses twice a month. The men carried them inside and set them in rows while the women greeted each other, laid out the food and looked after the children running to and fro.

Almost half of the congregation was made up of extended Bowman families. Isaac had four brothers and each of them had numerous sons and daughters. When a church group became too large to fit into a single home or barn, a new congregation would be formed, mostly of the younger married couples. The current group was made up of some twenty families and only about one hundred and twenty-five people. It would be a few years yet before they would need to split up.

John positioned his buggy among the others lined up across the hillside. He got out and unhitched his horse. While he led the mare to the corral where a dozen other buggy horses were already lined up and munching hay, Rebecca and her mother carried their baskets to the house. As she passed Samuel standing beside his father, she stopped and spoke quietly. "I saw someone buying birdhouses this morning. They took two."

"I'll tell Luke. He'll have to get busy and make more."

"Using the tree to display them was a good idea."

"I'm glad you think so."

Her mother frowned at her and motioned for her to come along. Rebecca ignored her. "How are your hands today? Are they still hurting you?"

"Not as much. Only when I bump them. Which happens a lot. They itch more now."

"The doctor said that meant they are healing. I see the bishop heading in. I'd better get this food inside."

"Will you be back at our place tomorrow?"

"I will."

The corner of his lip turned up in a little smile. *"Goot."*

It surprised her just how hard it was to walk away from him.

Although he had been reluctant to come, Samuel was glad he did. He enjoyed the three-hour-long service. It was familiar and comforting. He knew the drawn-out hymns by heart and didn't need to read the words from the *Ausbund*, their Amish hymnal, but he missed the weight of the large black book in his hands. Jonas Beachy, the bishop, was a good preacher. He and his two deacons spoke eloquently on the gathering in of the harvest and giving thanks for the bounty of the land.

Yet all the time Samuel sat on the hard backless bench or knelt on the floor, his mind constantly slipped back to when he sat beside Rebecca in the coolness of the night. It seemed that she was always on his mind these days. He listened for her voice among the singers and picked it out easily. It was the sweet alto that he had come to know while she was working in the house. She sang or hummed to let him know where she was ever since he had asked her to. She was kind that way, always being available without being intrusive now that he was up and out of bed.

When the prayer meeting finally ended, he allowed Timothy to lead him outside. That was when the hard part started. He was soon surrounded by the men of the community. He had to retell the story of the explosion to his friends and cousins and answer their questions about his sight. He had to listen to their words of sympathy and nod when he just wanted to crawl into the buggy and go home. They all meant well, but he quickly grew tired of being the center of attention.

Noah stood at his side. "We can go in and eat now. Do you want to come in or would you rather wait out here?"

He wasn't about to have everyone watch him be fed like an infant. "I'll wait out here. Just put me in the shade somewhere."

Noah led him to a set of steps at the side of the house and then went to get his meal. Thankful to be left alone, he relaxed for a few minutes. The sounds of a Sunday gathering poured through the air around him. The clatter of plates, tableware and conversation came from inside the house behind him. He must be near an open window. He listened to the voices and could pick out his *Onkel* Roy and his father discussing the corn harvest and the weather. From across the lawn, he heard the shrieks and laughter of the youngest children playing tag. Soon, his father and his cronies would get up a game of quoits once the midday meal was finished. His mother would be among the women cleaning up inside. When they were done, they would gather in rockers and lawn chairs in the shade and catch up on all the news.

A few of the young people would slip off to the barn, where they would stand in awkward groups with the boys in one pack and the maidens in the other until someone brought them together with a game of volleyball or baseball. A few would be missing. Those would be making dates for later that evening. Many a young man came to church in his open buggy with the hopes of convincing one special girl to ride home with him after the singing that evening.

Unlike his brothers, Samuel had never been among that group. His focus had always been on making sure the family business became successful. He knew he had earned a reputation of being stuck up among his peers, but he knew a family of his own would have to wait.

Had he waited too long? If he had chosen a wife, he would have had someone to look after him now instead of burdening his parents. Someone like Rebecca.

Before long, he heard footsteps approaching. He assumed it was Noah coming back. "I'm not hungry so don't worry about a plate for me."

"I thought you might not want to eat in front of others so I brought you a milk shake," Rebecca said as she sat down beside him. "It's chocolate. It will tide you over until you get home. You should be able to hold the glass yourself. It's plastic so it won't break it if it slips away, and it has a lid with a straw so you can't spill it."

"You think of everything."

"I try."

She pressed the glass between his bandaged hands

and he was able to hold it. He located the straw and drew a deep sip of the creamy cold drink. "It's *goot*."

"I like strawberry better myself. Do you need anything else before I go?"

For you to stay awhile. He didn't say it out loud.

"Noah is coming. I'll see you in the morning." She rose and he heard her move away.

His brother plopped down by his feet. "I brought you a plate. Do you want me to feed you or should I get mother?"

"Rebecca brought me a milk shake. You can have my plate, too."

"*Wunderbarr. Aenti* Edna gave me the last slice of her *snitz* and made me promise to give it to you. Are you sure you don't want it?"

Their aunt's dried apple pie was one of Noah's favorite treats. Samuel smiled. "You can have it."

"*Danki.* What were you and Rebecca talking about?"

"Nothing special. She just stopped by to give this milk shake."

"That was kind of her. I'm glad the two of you are getting along so well."

"What do you mean by that?"

"Just that you didn't seem to like her when she first came, and now you do."

He did like her. More than he wanted to. "She's bossy. I don't care for bossy women. They should be humble and quiet-spoken."

Noah chuckled. "Like *Mamm*?"

"Point taken. *Mamm* might be opinionated at home, but she is always demure in public."

"So is Rebecca."

"I guess I never noticed."

YOUR PARTICIPATION IS REQUESTED!

Dear Reader,

Since you are a lover of our books – we would like to get to know you!

Inside you will find a short Reader's Survey. Sharing your answers with us will help our editorial staff understand who you are and what activities you enjoy.

To thank you for your participation, we would like to send you 2 books and 2 gifts – **ABSOLUTELY FREE!**

Enjoy your gifts with our appreciation,

Pam Powers

SEE INSIDE FOR READER'S SURVEY

For Your Reading Pleasure...

FREE!

We'll send you 2 books and 2 gifts
ABSOLUTELY FREE
just for completing our Reader's Survey!

YOUR READER'S SURVEY
"THANK YOU" FREE GIFTS INCLUDE:
- ► 2 FREE books
- ► 2 lovely surprise gifts

PLEASE FILL IN THE CIRCLES COMPLETELY TO RESPOND

1) What type of fiction books do you enjoy reading? (Check all that apply)
- ○ Suspense/Thrillers
- ○ Action/Adventure
- ○ Modern-day Romances
- ○ Historical Romance
- ○ Humour
- ○ Paranormal Romance

2) What attracted you most to the last fiction book you purchased on impulse?
- ○ The Title
- ○ The Cover
- ○ The Author
- ○ The Story

3) What is usually the greatest influencer when you <u>plan</u> to buy a book?
- ○ Advertising
- ○ Referral
- ○ Book Review

4) How often do you access the internet?
- ○ Daily
- ○ Weekly
- ○ Monthly
- ○ Rarely or never.

5) How many NEW paperback fiction novels have you purchased in the past 3 months?
- ○ 0 - 2
- ○ 3 - 6
- ○ 7 or more

YES! I have completed the Reader's Survey. Please send me the 2 FREE books and 2 FREE gifts (gifts are worth about $10) for which I qualify. I understand that I am under no obligation to purchase any books, as explained on the back of this card.

❏ I prefer the regular-print edition
105/305 IDL GH5X

❏ I prefer the larger-print edition
122/322 IDL GH5X

FIRST NAME	LAST NAME

ADDRESS

APT.#	CITY

STATE/PROV.

ZIP/POSTAL CODE

The sound of running feet approached and thudded to a stop in front of them. "We're getting up a game of volleyball, Noah. Want to join us? I picked you for my team already." The breathless female voice belonged to their neighbor's daughter Fanny.

"I can't today."

Samuel took a sip of his drink to keep from laughing. Noah couldn't have sounded more disappointed if he tried.

"Oh. Okay. I'll see you later. Are you staying for the singing tonight?"

"I don't know if I can. It all depends."

"Sarah Hochstetler is going to be there tonight. She turned sixteen last week and this will be her first one. She has her eye on you, but some fella might steal her away if you don't make a move soon," Fanny teased.

"She does?"

"She's on my volleyball team. You could make a good impression if you came and played with us."

"It doesn't matter. I have to stay here."

"All right. It was good to see you, Samuel. I hope you get better soon."

"*Danki*, Fanny." Samuel heard the sound of her running away. Fanny seldom moved at half speed.

Noah sighed, and Samuel took pity on his brother. "You don't need to babysit me. Go have fun with your friends."

"Are you sure? *Mamm* said I was to stay here and watch out for you."

"I'm sure. Go on. Impress Sarah Hochstetler with your skill and charm." Was his baby brother old enough to be chasing after a young *maedel*? It didn't seem possible.

"You're the best." Noah took off as if he was afraid Samuel would change his mind. Or maybe he was afraid their mother would catch wind of his desertion.

Samuel sat back and waited for Rebecca. Was she watching?

Rebecca couldn't believe it when she saw Noah take off after Fanny Erb, leaving Samuel all alone. She waited a full minute until she realized Noah had joined the volleyball game getting underway. He had no intention of keeping an eye on Samuel. She turned to her mother. "Excuse me. I must see if Samuel needs anything."

"Dear, you aren't working today. Let his family look after him."

"I'm not doing it because it's my job. I'm doing it out of Christian charity." She knew her mother couldn't argue against that.

She crossed the strip of lawn just as a pair of rowdy boys chasing each other around the house barreled into Samuel.

The two young boys apologized profusely and then took off. Samuel had one bandaged hand pressed to the side of his face. She rushed forward. "Samuel, are you hurt?"

"I don't think so. I wasn't expecting to be blindsided. Who were they?"

She sat down beside him in relief. "Fanny Erb's two youngest brothers."

"The whole family runs faster than the horses they raise."

She chuckled. "I think the horses have more sense. Are you sure you aren't hurt?"

"Is there any blood?"

She examined him closely. *"Nee."*

"Then I'm fine except for a few new bruises."

She heard the door of the house open and saw his father come out followed by the bishop. "Your father and the bishop are coming this way."

"Samuel, it is good to see you are well enough to attend the services," the bishop said. Rebecca rose and stepped a few feet away, making room for the men to sit down beside Samuel on the steps.

"God was merciful to me. My eyes are closed, but he left my ears open so that I might hear your good preaching."

Did she detect a note of sarcasm? Was he still angry at God? None of the others seemed to notice.

Isaac wrapped his hands around his knee. "The bishop and I have decided on a day for the workshop raising. Everyone should be done with the harvest by next church day. We will hold it the following Thursday."

"That should give everyone enough time to finish their own work," the bishop said. "Is that agreeable to you?"

"If it is okay with my father, it's fine with me." Samuel's lips flattened as a muscle twitched in his jaw.

"*Goot.* We will have your wood shop open again in no time." The bishop patted Samuel's knee and rose to his feet. "Isaac, will you join me for a game of quoits?"

"I was thinking you might want to play someone who doesn't beat you so badly," Isaac said with a twinkle in his eye.

The bishop straightened and fisted his hands on his

hips. "There's a challenge I can't refuse. Get ready to eat those words."

The two men walked away, and Rebecca sat down beside Samuel again. "You must have faith that you'll be able to return to the work you love. All things are possible with God."

"That's the day the dealer from Cincinnati was to come and look at my work. All he would find now is a pile of ashes."

"When your eyes and hands have healed you will show him your best work."

"If I worked for six months, I wouldn't be able to build all the furniture that was lost in the fire. Without money to buy new lumber and new machinery, I couldn't do it, anyway. Besides, when Timothy spoke to Mr. Clark on the phone after the fire, the man mentioned he had other woodworkers he intended to visit that week. He will place his contracts elsewhere. He has a business to run."

"Then you will find another dealer who will buy your furniture at a fair price, and you will not need Mr. Clark's money. When God closes a door, He opens a window."

"And sometimes He's telling us we can't have what we want," he said bitterly.

"Sometimes, He asks us to pay attention to His plan and not our own," she added softly.

"If His plan is to scatter my brothers by sending them elsewhere to find work, then I don't think much of it. I have to accept that my risk resulted in failure. Would you get Luke or Timothy for me? I'd like to go home now."

He stood and moved back to lean against the house

with his arms folded protectively across his chest. She had little choice but to do as he asked. She found his brothers by the barn talking with a group of young men their age. A few of them had short beards indicating they were recently married. Most, like the Bowman brothers were clean-shaven. She paused beside them. "Samuel would like to go home now. Could one of you arrange to take him?"

A young man beside Luke spoke up. "I brought my open buggy today. I can take him."

"I'll go with you," Luke said. "He can't be left alone for long."

"Danki." Rebecca smiled at the group. As they left to hitch up the buggy, she started back toward the house.

Timothy followed her. "Is Samuel feeling poorly?"

She stopped walking. "Your father and the bishop chose the day for the wood shop raising. It will be on the same day Samuel had planned for Mr. Clark to visit."

"And it reminded him he has nothing left to show for all his months of hard work." Timothy's eyes filled with understanding as he gazed toward Samuel standing alone.

"It was your work that went up in smoke, too." She didn't sense any bitterness in Timothy. Was it only Samuel who struggled to come to grips with the loss?

"My brother believes he's the only one who can hold the family together. He doesn't realize each of us must make that decision for ourselves."

"Would his plan have worked if not for the fire?"

"Probably. Samuel is a fine craftsman, but he can't run a big business alone. Until he accepts that, he's going to drive us away even if there is work to keep us here."

She thought of her beautiful table at home and the

lovely Bible cabinet where her great-great-grandfather's Bible was displayed. There were examples of the Bowman's fine craftsmanship all across the county. It was a shame the Cincinnati dealer couldn't see them.

A sudden thought occurred to her. Why couldn't he see them? "Timothy, would you stay if the workshop reopened?"

"If I could earn enough to support a family, *ja*."

She looked over the community gathered in groups, chatting and enjoying their day of rest amid the stunning fall colors of the hills around them. She smiled and rubbed her chin. "Timothy, I have an idea."

"Okay, do I get to hear it?"

Luke was leading Samuel toward his friend's waiting buggy. "Let's share it with Samuel and Luke. It will take everyone's cooperation."

She reached Samuel's side just as he climbed in and sat down. She grabbed the door before Luke could close it. "Samuel, I have an idea how we can show your furniture dealer the kind of work you can do."

"Rebecca, stop. That dream is over. It's gone. I don't want to talk about it anymore. Luke, get me home."

She touched his arm. "But you haven't heard what I have to say."

He pulled away. "Don't you know when to stop talking? It's over. What are you waiting for, Luke? Take me home!"

Defeated, she stepped back and allowed the carriage to roll away. He wouldn't even listen to her.

Chapter Eight

Samuel regretted his rudeness to Rebecca before he had gone half a mile. His failure was no fault of hers. She deserved to be treated with respect.

The following morning, his brothers and his father had all gone out to the fields before she arrived. He was seated at the kitchen table listening with half an ear as his mother read the morning paper to him.

"Good morning, Anna. Samuel." The flat way she said his name was his first clue that he was still in trouble.

His mother turned the page of the newspaper. "Hello, Rebecca. Would you finish reading to Samuel while I start my laundry?"

"I'll do the laundry. You keep reading, Anna." He heard the door to the basement bang shut. Was she avoiding him?

After his mother finished the paper, Samuel fumbled his way to the washroom downstairs. "Rebecca, may I talk to you?"

"I'm busy." She brushed past him and dashed up the stairs.

He found out it was easy for her to play hide-and-seek with a blind man. After following her several places only to be left standing alone, he gave in.

"I'll be going to my room now," he announced in the kitchen. He wasn't sure anyone heard him until his mother replied.

"That's fine."

He left the room feeling like a fool. How hard was it to apologize to one woman? And why was he trying so hard?

He settled in upstairs, but couldn't find a comfortable spot in bed. He wasn't tired. He was bored and he was getting angry. Rebecca had been hired to take care of him, not avoid him.

Time dragged by. Being idle chafed. His entire life had been taken up with work, with doing more and doing it better so that the family could reap the benefits of his labors. It felt as if it had all been for nothing.

Rising, he paced the small confines of his room for a while, and then fell back into bed with his arm over his face.

Sometime later, Rebecca spoke from his doorway. "Your mother has asked that I take the lunches out to the men. I thought you might like to walk along with me. It's a crisp morning."

So she was finally speaking to him. "Why not? There's certainly nothing to do in here."

She led the way outdoors. She waited until he made it down the porch steps. "Your mother told me they were cutting corn by the old railroad. I'm not familiar with where that is."

Her cool tone said more than her words. She was still upset. Their merry chase had erased his desire to apologize. He could be cool, too. "The old section of railroad tracks runs along the river behind the barn. I can hear the corn binder from here."

"Then your hearing is better than mine. Will you be comfortable walking with your hand on my shoulder? I'm afraid I need both my hands to carry these lunch pails."

He couldn't maintain this indifference if he was touching her. "Maybe I should stay here."

"Now that you've made an effort to get outside, I think you should enjoy a little of this glorious weather." Her softened tone held a hint of an overture.

He really didn't want to go back in the house.

"I know it's frightening to think of walking so far. I promise to go slow so you won't trip over anything, but I would like to deliver these meals before they get cold."

The corner of his mouth ticked up. "I'm not frightened. I trust you."

He did. Implicitly.

She placed his hand on her shoulder. "I'd be scared if I were in your shoes. Then again, if I were in your shoes I would be tripping over everything because they would be miles too big for me."

"Do you make a joke out of everything?"

"Not everything. It's just better to laugh than it is to cry."

They walked in silence for a while. He had to adjust his stride to her short steps, but they soon reached the cornfield where his family was working. He didn't need his eyes to tell him what was going on. It was a task he had helped with since he was a child.

His father would be driving the corn binder. A small gasoline-powered engine mounted on the side of the cutter operated the blades while a team of horses pulled the machine along as it sliced the cornstalks off at the base. A special belt lifted bundles of stalks up to a second flatbed wagon. One of his brothers would be driving a team alongside the cutter while the other brother had the dirty job of gathering the cornstalks and piling them at the back of the wagon. Many an argument had been started about who got to drive and whose turn it was to catch.

When the catch wagon was overflowing with cornstalks, the driver would turn the team away and head for the silo. A second wagon would move up and take its place. Only one person was needed to drive the loaded wagon back to the silo, so one of the brothers would hop off and race to jump on the new wagon. Once there, he took over the reins or began catching. The process would be repeated flawlessly each time the wagon was full. The corn cutter never had to stop as long as the wagons were emptied and returned in a timely fashion.

Rebecca came to a halt. "I think the corn stubble is too rough for you to walk through. I'll have you stay here."

"Not a problem." He squatted on his heels to wait for her return. At least they were speaking to each other again.

"Will your father stop for me?"

Samuel nodded. "He'll stop the corn binder for a brief lunch as long as the weather looks favorable. If there is a threat of rain, my *daed* will eat standing up and driving the team until he gets his crop in or it's too dark to see."

"My father used to say rain is the friend of the plants and the enemy of the harvest."

"It's true. If the corn stored in the silos is too damp, it will mold and rot. The moisture content of the plants has to be just right to maximize the nutrition the cows will get from their feed over the long cold winter months."

"He's waving for me to come out. I'll be back as quick as I can."

"Rebecca, I'm sorry I was abrupt with you yesterday." He waited tensely for her reply.

"You are forgiven, Samuel. I can be pushy sometimes."

"I appreciate that you want to help, but I know what needs to be done. I'll take care of it as soon as I'm healed."

"I know you will."

Her voice carried more confidence in him than he felt. She believed in him. Somehow, he would find a way to make things right.

Rebecca was pleased with Samuel's steady improvement over the next few days. He rarely spent time in his room, preferring instead to be out of doors. Although the tasks he could perform were limited, he did manage to help his mother by waiting on customers at the gift shop. He even devised a way to sweep the floor by having Rebecca tie towels to his shoes so he could slide his feet across the wide planks while she dusted the shelves. He still refused to eat with the family. Timothy and his father were the only ones he allowed to help him with that since he still had to be fed.

On Wednesday evening, she went home to do her own housekeeping. Bright and early the next morning, she returned to the Bowman farm. As her horse trotted through the covered bridge, a growing sense of joy enveloped her. She was happy to be a part of this family, even for a short time. Being with Samuel was the reason her spirits soared higher each day.

Anna was busy in the kitchen washing glass canning jars and barely glanced Rebecca's way when she came in. Samuel normally sat at the kitchen table this time of day while his mother read the morning paper to him, but he wasn't around.

"*Guder mariye*, Anna. Where is Samuel?"

"He hasn't come down."

That was odd. "What can I do to help this morning?"

"I have a bucket of fresh dug potatoes on the back porch. If you would wash them and leave them to dry, that would be great. I'll pack them into paper bags later and take them down to the store when I go."

Glancing around, Rebecca noticed a large pail of apples on the table. "Would you like me to take these apples down to the store for you, too?"

"*Nee*, I've already taken down the good ones I plan to sell today. These are for applesauce. I have to start canning soon. The fruit will be falling on the ground before long."

Rebecca nodded in sympathy. The early days of autumn were the busiest time of the year for Amish housewives. Gathering in the harvest meant a steady stream of vegetables and fruit to preserve on top of the daily chores, cooking for harvest crews and working beside the men in the fields when needed. Spare minutes were few and far between.

After washing and arranging the potatoes on racks to dry, Rebecca went back inside. Samuel still wasn't up. Today was the day she needed to change his dressing, so perhaps he was reluctant to make an appearance. "I'm going to check on Samuel."

"Okay." Anna didn't look up from her task of coring apples.

Samuel was sitting at the desk by the window. He tensed when she knocked. "*Guder mariye*, Samuel. How are you this morning?"

"I've been dreading your appearance."

"You certainly know how to flatter a woman." She saw the tiniest hint of a smile before it fled.

"You know what I meant."

"This time it won't be so painful."

"And how can you know that?" His derisive tone signaled his disbelief.

"You said your hands have been itching. That means healing."

He extended them palms up on the table. "We might as well get it over with."

"Did you take your pain medication?"

"I did."

"I'm amazed."

"I learned my lesson at the doctor's office."

Rebecca left to collect her supplies and returned five minutes later with a box of bandages, a large basin of warm water, liquid soap and the latex gloves the doctor had given her. She set them all on the desk along with a towel and pulled on the gloves. Using a pair of sewing scissors, she began cutting away the old dressings on his right hand. When she was down to the last layer, she guided his hand to the basin. "Soak it for a few minutes. Have I hurt you yet?"

"Not enough to mention."

"I'm thankful for that."

"So am I."

After a few minutes, she unfolded a towel and spread it out. "Lift your hand out of the water. How is it?"

"Stinging."

Gently she removed the last layer of bandages to reveal his reddened skin and peeling blisters. Some areas of his palm were bright red while others were a ruddy brown indicating old skin that had yet to slough. She began lightly wiping the entire palm, trying not to scrub.

"How does it look?"

"Not bad."

"You don't lie very well."

"It looks painful, but I don't think there is as much swelling." She applied some soap and began massaging his hand in slow circles trying to loosen the dead skin.

She had never noticed how long and supple his fingers were. They weren't soft or weak. Even injured, she could feel the underlying strength in his wrist and arm. He had hands made to craft delicate designs into hard wood and smooth the rough edges until the oak or cherry felt like satin to the touch. He had skilled craftsman's hands and she liked the feel of them. The simple task of washing his injuries took on a whole new meaning. This was the way a wife might touch her husband.

He inhaled sharply and her gaze flew to his face. "What's wrong?"

He'd never had a woman hold his hand and caress it with such tenderness. The sensation, aside from the mild pain, was a disturbing one. Her hands were small and delicate, and yet they were strong, too. The fragrance of her lavender soap filled his senses, and he knew the scent would forever remind him of this moment.

"I'm sorry if I'm hurting you," she said softly. There was a breathless quality to her voice that sent his pulse soaring.

If only he knew for certain that his vision would return. Then he might have the right to speak about the affection growing in his heart. Until then, it was best to remain silent and pretend her touch was like any other.

"You're doing okay, but can we speed it up?" He didn't know how much longer he could keep a lid on his emotions.

"Of course." She rinsed and dried his hand and applied the antibiotic cream the doctor had prescribed. Samuel pulled away from her and propped his elbow on the table while she repeated the procedure on his other hand.

In his mind, he worked out the dimensions of a new shop and the placement of the equipment he hoped to purchase one day down to the smallest detail. It kept him from thinking about how much he wished he could see her face. Was she being the dutiful nurse or did she feel this connection, too, this pull toward each other?

Finally, she was done. "There. That wasn't so bad, was it?"

"It all depends on your definition of *bad.*"

"Are you ready to have me do your face, or would you rather take a break?"

Her hands on his face? No, he wasn't going to endure that. "I'll let Timothy do it this evening."

"Oh. Are you sure? I don't mind." She sounded disappointed.

"Wrap my hands and then go help my mother. I'm sure she has something for you to do."

"Samuel, I was hired to take care of you."

"And you have. I'm getting up and around without much trouble. I feel stronger now that I'm eating solid food. You have helped immensely. Once these dressings come off my eyes, I won't need you at all."

"That is the day I pray for," she said softly.

"As do I."

She wrapped his hands and taped the ends of the bandages. "I haven't used as much gauze because the drainage is much less. Can you move your fingers?"

He tried and was able to press his first two fingers against his thumbs without undue pain. "That's better. I'll be able to hold my own spoon and fork now. Timothy will be overjoyed."

"You can join the family for supper tonight."

"I'd rather have one evening of practice up here before I risk pouring soup down my chin in front of everyone."

She giggled. "I'll be sure and send up extra towels with your tray."

Her laughter was a balm to his spirit. If only he could judge her interest in him. Was there a shadow of hope that she held him in affection? He had heard that the eyes were windows into the soul. He wanted to gaze into her eyes and see if she smiled from within when she looked at him. "*Danki*, Rebecca. You were right. It was much less painful."

"I could read the paper to you before I go and help your mother."

He didn't want her to go. Any excuse to keep her close was one he liked. The sound of her voice would soothe him and make the long hours of the morning bearable. "That would be nice."

"*Wunderbarr.* Let me put away these supplies and I'll be right back with the paper."

Her footsteps hurried away and he had a chance to draw a full breath. It didn't help. The scent of lavender still lingered in the air. He stood and took a turn around the room. What was he doing? Why was he thinking romantic thoughts about Rebecca Miller? She was a widow who still mourned her husband.

Although he'd known her for years, Samuel couldn't recall her face clearly. What had triggered this sudden interest in her? Nothing she had said or done. Pouring water on a sick man's feet wasn't romantic in the least.

She was bossy and opinionated. She wasn't the kind of woman he imagined would interest him. The sound of her hurrying up the stairs reached him and he sat down.

She breezed into the room. "I found the paper."

He heard her chair scrape back and he knew she had taken a seat across from him. What would she look like with the morning sunlight pouring across her fair skin? "Samuel, you're flushed all of the sudden. Do you feel all right?"

Before he could form a reply, her hand cupped his cheek and neck below his ear where he wasn't burned or bandaged. Her fingers were damp and cool. He froze, not wanting her to see how much she affected him. "I feel fine."

"You aren't feverish, but your voice sounds raspy. Maybe the paper can wait until you've had a rest. I'll come back later." She withdrew her hand.

He leaned away and folded his arms over his chest. "Don't go. I want to hear what's going on. Read."

"Very well."

In her low musical voice, the first thing he had liked about her, she read the front page news about traffic improvements the county was hoping to make. After that, she went on to weather reports and the hog and corn market news. It was amazing anyone could make the hog market reports sound interesting and soothing, but she did. By the end of half an hour, she had covered the entire paper from the local ball games and highlights to the specials at the grocery store in Berlin.

The paper rustled as she closed it. "That's all for now."

The appetizing smell of simmering apples had overpowered the scent of lavender in the room. "*Mamm* must be making applesauce. Maybe I'll sneak a few apple slices when she isn't looking."

"Would you like me to distract her for you?"

"I think I can manage on my own."

"I'll slip you one or two if you can't."

"It's a deal." He chuckled as they made their way downstairs.

"I was wondering if you two were ever coming down. I was about to come up and check on you." His mother's words held a hint of reproach.

"Rebecca read the paper to me. She said you were busy." He found the table and sat down.

"That was kind of you, Rebecca. I can't get away from this applesauce for another hour or two. Would you mind opening the store for me? If anyone comes in just write down what they buy. There is a cash box under the counter. It has enough money in it to make change."

"I'm sure I can manage."

"Do you want me to keep you company?" he offered.

"*Nee*, keep your mother company. I'll be fine by myself. I'll take those potatoes with me," Rebecca said quickly. Too, quickly.

He had the feeling he had missed something. When she was gone, his mother didn't beat around the bush. "Samuel, you are a grown fellow, and I should not have to have this conversation with you."

He sat up straighter. "What conversation?"

"Rebecca is a single woman. You risk her reputation by treating her with such ease in your company. You are much improved. It is unseemly now for her to spend time in your room."

"We have done nothing wrong. She changed my dressings and read the paper. What harm is there in that?"

"None, but such familiarity can lead to temptations."

Hadn't he already discovered that for himself? "I would not harm Rebecca's reputation for anything. She has been kindness itself to me."

"I like her, too. Very much. If you should decide to ask her out I would approve."

He squirmed in his seat. "I didn't say I wanted to go out with her."

"Silly boy, you don't have to say those things. A mother has eyes and ears. Not much goes on in this house that I don't know about. Remember that."

Later that week, Rebecca once again took Samuel to the doctor's office. He tolerated the long trip much better the second time and remembered to take his pain medication before they arrived. At the office, she remained in the waiting room while Samuel was taken back to an exam room.

"How are you doing, Samuel?" the doctor asked when he was finished with his initial examination.

"Better every day." Physically it was true, but the worry about his family's future never left him.

"Any problems? Any signs of infection?"

Samuel shook his head. "Rebecca Miller and my brother Timothy are taking good care of me."

"I thought you must be doing well. Rebecca would have let me know if there was a problem. Let me get these dressings off and have a look for myself."

Samuel waited as the doctor unwrapped his hands. He made only a few noncommittal noises. "They feel better. There is less pain."

"I'm impressed and pleased with your progress. There seems to be very little scarring considering the extent of the burns. You can leave the wraps off soon. There are a few places that still look raw, but letting them dry out may be best. Now, let's take a look at your face. I'm going to dim the lights. Let me know if they're still too bright."

Samuel tensed as he waited for the doctor to remove the bandages from his eyes. If his hands were healing, his eyes were healing, too. They had to be.

"This looks good. Your eyebrows and your eyelashes will grow back. Your eyelids are still raw looking, but that's to be expected. All right, open your eyes slowly. Stop if it hurts."

Samuel let his eyes flutter open. His heart began to hammer in his chest. "I can't see anything."

"Can you distinguish between light and dark?"

Samuel's throat tightened. "It's all dark. I don't see any light at all. Turn on the lights. Face me toward the window." His breath came in short, harsh gasps.

"I'm going to put some drops in your eyes and some light gauze pads over them. You won't need the heavy bandages anymore."

"Why can't I see? My burns were healing. Why can't I see?"

"There may be several reasons. In the event your vision hadn't improved today, I made an appointment for you to see the ophthalmologist I've been consulting with. He's a friend of mine. There won't be any cost for his examination and he can see you now. Would you like Rebecca to go with us?"

Samuel shook his head. This was something he needed to face alone. "Will it take long?"

"His office is fifteen minutes from here, and he has cleared his schedule to see you. If you don't feel up to doing this now, we can make it another time."

"I need to know what's wrong. Have someone tell Rebecca that I'll be back shortly."

The doctor wrapped a new bandage around Samuel's eyes. "Hopefully, Dr. Westbrook can give us some answers."

The doctor led Samuel outside and was helping him into his car when Samuel heard Rebecca's voice. "Wait up. I'm coming, too."

Samuel paused. "It's not necessary, Rebecca."

She opened the door to the backseat. "Your father is paying me to take care of you. He would not like it if I let you go alone. And we both know that your mother would have a fit. Please drive on, Doctor."

Although he would not have admitted it, Samuel was glad she was there.

At the ophthalmology clinic, Samuel endured a lengthy exam. The doctor put drops in his eyes. It made them burn, and Samuel had to resist the urge to rub them. His face was positioned in a holder. He was told to look right and look left and to stare straight ahead. Rebecca stood close beside him through it all. He was never more grateful for her stubborn streak.

While the doctors finished conferring, Samuel waited anxiously for their verdict. Finally, Dr. Westbrook sat down at Samuel's side. "I'm going to send you home with some special dark glasses. You don't have to keep the bandages on anymore."

"Will I be blind forever?" Samuel choked out the question.

"I'm afraid I can't tell you that."

"What can you tell us?" Rebecca asked.

"In a flash burn such as the one Samuel endured, the blink reflex is so quick that the eyes are almost always protected. His eyelids sustained burns, but the corneas of his eyes did not. There is no scarring or clouding. The muscles of the pupils respond appropriately to light and dark. The pressures in the eyes are normal and the retinas are both intact."

Samuel rubbed his itching palms on his pant legs. "What are you saying?"

Chapter Nine

"They're wrong! I don't wish to be blind. Why would they think such a thing?"

Rebecca glanced at Samuel's angry face as she drove him home from the doctor's office. It was the first time he'd spoken since they had been told his blindness wasn't caused by his injury. "They are men of science. They believe what they have told you. It's possible."

"*Nee*, I'm not *naerfich*."

"They didn't say you were crazy." She didn't want to believe it, either. Samuel was a strong, determined man, but he had suffered a great blow. Perhaps this was God's way of teaching him humility. She reached the Bowman driveway and turned in.

"I don't want my family to know this," he said quickly.

"Samuel, it can't be hidden. The doctor has asked for a meeting with your family so that he can explain this to them."

"He couldn't explain it to me."

"You weren't willing to listen." She hated seeing him so tormented.

"You think I'm crazy, too."

"Far from it. I think you are upset and angry. When you are calm, you can hear what Dr. Marksman was trying to tell you. This was not your choice. This was your mind's reaction to a horrible trauma." She pulled the buggy to a stop beside the barn. She got out and went round to help him down.

He brushed past her and took a few steps away until he came up against the corral fence. He raised his fists to the sky. "Why do you allow this, God? I have prayed every day and every night that You will restore my sight. Why won't You let me see?"

Rebecca laid a hand on his shoulder. "I think you are asking the wrong question, Samuel."

"I don't know what you mean." Frustrated to the point of screaming, Samuel held on to his last ounce of sanity. She didn't understand. How could she?

"Maybe the question you should be asking yourself is what does God *want* you to see?"

He gripped the fence rail in front of him making his tender hands throb with pain. "I can't see anything!"

"Maybe that's because you aren't looking in the right direction. We must use faith, not our eyes to see what God asks of us. Try looking inward, Samuel."

"You're babbling."

"I'm going to visit my mother for a few hours. Tell Anna I won't be here for supper."

He bowed his head on his hands and heard her climb in the buggy and drive away. He listened a while longer. She wouldn't leave him out here alone, would she?

"Rebecca?"

Silence answered him. He was alone. Alone and afraid on his own farm. He had been brought low. Lower than he ever imagined he could feel. The hopelessness was like a bottomless pit yawning at his feet. One step and he could drop into it forever.

"Is this what you want me to see, Lord? That I'm not a strong man? That I'm nothing more than a frightened child?"

He leaned his forehead against the wooden fence. The board was solid and smooth and still held the warmth of the late-afternoon sun. Would the sunset be a pretty one tonight? When was the last time he paid attention to the color of the clouds at dusk? Years, maybe. How could he have known he'd never see another one.

"I will never ignore another of Your wonders, if You'll let me see them again. What do I have to offer You, Lord? What is worthy of such a gift?"

Nothing. He had nothing to offer. He could promise anything. He could promise to use his gifts to aid others, to be kinder to his brothers, to devote his life to praising God, but they were all things he believed he was already doing. What more did God want from him?

Was this how Luke felt when he lost his way? Did he see an abyss of despair and reach for drugs to keep from falling into it?

Samuel had always seen Luke's addiction as a weakness. Was this something they shared, like the color of their eyes?

He couldn't accept that. He wouldn't.

Rebecca said he was asking the wrong questions. *Okay, Lord, I won't ask why me. What do You want from me? Show me. I may not see, but I can listen to You. I'm listening, Lord. I'm listening.*

"Did your little nurse leave you out here all alone?"

Samuel straightened at the sound of Luke's voice. The clip-clop of horse's hooves told him his brother was returning with a team from the field. "It appears she did."

"That's not like her. Do you…do you need some help?" His brother's tentative offer made Samuel realize how often he had rejected Luke's help in the past.

"*Danki*, but I can figure out where the house is."

"Nice shades, by the way. How is your vision? Can you see now?"

Samuel touched the dark glasses that wrapped around his face. "Not yet."

"Give it some time. Your hands look awful. Do they hurt?"

Pushing away from the fence, Samuel flexed his fingers. His hands were still stiff and tender, but he was ready to do some work with them. "Which team do you have?"

"Oscar and Dutch."

"Would you like some help rubbing them down?"

"Sure. If you think you can."

"I can brush a horse in my sleep. We all can. I reckon I can do it without looking." Samuel reached out until his fingers came in contact with the mane of the nearest horse. He held on tight. "Lead the way."

He walked beside his brother and waited outside the stall as Luke unharnessed the pair. Samuel felt along the bench by the wall until he located the currycomb and brush they kept on pegs.

"Do you want Oscar, or do you want Dutch?" Luke asked.

"Either."

"This is Oscar." Luke guided Samuel to the horse's side.

Once he started the task he had done since he was

a small boy, Samuel forgot for a few minutes that he couldn't see. He didn't need his eyes to let his hand glide the brush over the big draft horse's shiny dappled-gray coat. He drew a deep breath and let the familiar barn smells of horses, hay and old timbers fill his lungs.

"What did you say to Rebecca to make her run off and leave you?" Luke asked.

"Why do you assume it was something I said?" Samuel worked his way along one side of the horse.

"Call it an educated guess."

Samuel chuckled. "It usually is me doing the scolding."

"That's what I meant. So?"

"I was bemoaning my plight. Railing against God for taking my sight."

"I can see why you would. I'm sorry this happened to you, Samuel."

"Rebecca has less sympathy." He walked around the horse's rump and began brushing his other side.

"She's a very wise woman."

Samuel heard the respect in his brother's voice and wondered if Luke's feelings for Rebecca were deeper than friendship. "She is wise and single. Is she someone you might consider courting?"

He held his breath waiting for Luke's answer. As much as he cared for Rebecca himself, he wouldn't stand in the way of someone else, especially Luke, if he had similar feelings.

Luke laughed heartily. Samuel frowned. "I don't see what you think is funny."

"Are you offering to step aside if I'm interested?"

"I don't need to step aside. Rebecca was hired to help with my care until the harvest was over. It's nearly done. I'm just curious if you like her in that way?" He brushed harder as he reached Oscar's shoulder.

"I like her fine, but she only has eyes for you."

"What?" He paused and cocked his head. Had he heard Luke right? Oscar swung his head around to nip as he sometimes did, but Samuel blocked him with an elbow to the nose.

"Samuel, what did you just do?"

"Oscar was going to bite me and I elbowed him. What do you mean Rebecca only has eyes for me?"

"You saw Oscar swinging his head around?"

"*Nee*, I can't see anything. I just knew he was going to do it. I'm not foolish enough to think Rebecca would be interested in a blind man. You're wrong about that." Samuel finished brushing the horse and felt his way out of the stall. He tossed the brush and comb onto the bench.

Luke came to his side and laid a hand on his shoulder. "She cares for you a lot, Samuel. A man doesn't need eyes to hear the softness in her voice when she speaks to you or to notice that she is always at your side when you need something. She teases a smile from you when you are down. She makes you do more than you think you can."

"She's a fine nurse. That's all."

"I'm not blind. When I see Rebecca gazing at you, I see a woman who just might be falling for you. What you do with that information is up to you."

Rebecca sat at her mother's table in her bright and airy kitchen. A long row of windows let the late-afternoon light pour in. Pulling a pan of roast chicken with vegetables from the oven, her mother placed it on the stovetop. "I thought about inviting John to join us. What do you think?"

Rebecca frowned. "I don't want to invite John to supper. I'm not sure I want to stay for supper if I'm going to be lectured through the entire meal about what a catch he is."

"Rebecca May, do not speak to your mother in such a tone!"

Reining in her resentment, Rebecca sighed. "I'm sorry, *Mamm*. I'm tired tonight. It's been a long week. It is your home, and you may invite John if you wish."

"What has you so upset, daughter?" She checked the vegetables and chicken for doneness with a fork.

Rebecca decided there was no point in denying it. "Samuel Bowman."

Her mother spun to face her. "Why? What has he done?"

"It's not what he has done. It's what he won't do."

"This sounds like it may require a pot of tea to solve. Shall I put some on? This chicken needs another twenty minutes."

"I'll get it. You finish what you're doing." Rebecca busied herself getting the tea ready. When it was done, she carried the mugs to the table where her mother was already seated.

Her mother picked up her mug with both hands and took a sip. The steam rose and fogged her glasses until she moved the cup away. "So, tell me what Samuel won't do."

"He won't let go of his anger at God for his injury."

"God has broad shoulders. He can bear our anger for He is the one who gave us our emotions. Samuel is a good man. He will realize the error of his thinking in time and turn to God for forgiveness."

"I pray that you are right."

"I am. This is a hard thing to bear for a strong young man. What does the doctor say about his eyes?"

"That his blindness isn't due to his injury. It is his mind that won't allow him to see. The doctor is hopeful Samuel will recover, but I'm afraid he will give up and stop trying."

"As Walter stopped trying to get better?" her mother asked quietly.

Rebecca's throat closed and she could only nod.

"You have come to care for Samuel a great deal, haven't you?"

"I shouldn't, I know. I'm trying to control my feelings."

"Any why shouldn't you care for him?"

"I loved my husband. I don't want to love another man."

"Well, then, it is best that you don't."

"*Mamm*, why do you say that? You are forever pushing John at me."

Her mother stirred her tea. "That was when I thought you might fall in love again. If you are determined to stop trying, then I'm wasting my time."

"Is that what I'm doing?" If she refused to accept that she could love another, then love would never come her way.

"I think you can answer that question better than I can. Our negative thoughts can become self-fulfilling prophecies."

Tears sprang to Rebecca's eyes and rolled down her

cheeks. How could she profess to believe in God's plan when she was so angry herself?

"I'm no better than Samuel. He doesn't want to see. I don't want to love. The truth is I'm as mad at God for taking Walter away as Samuel is at his loss of sight. We are a sad pair."

Her mother came and wrapped her arms around Rebecca's shoulders. "A sad pair, perhaps, but neither of you is beyond hope. God heals all wounds in time. Here on earth or in the hereafter."

"I don't know why I'm so upset. I like Samuel and I want to see him get well. That's all. I want all my patients to get well. I'm grateful God has given me this calling. Caring for others is fulfilling work. I believe it is the path God has chosen for me. I'm content with that."

Her mother tipped her head to the side and regarded her with pity. "Rebecca, who are you trying to convince?"

Rebecca woke suddenly in the middle of the night. She lay still in the darkness listening for Samuel's footsteps overhead. She had learned when she returned from visiting her mother that Samuel had retreated to his room, refused supper and wouldn't speak to anyone.

Rebecca had fallen asleep listening to the sounds of him pacing overhead. Now it was quiet. Was he finally sleeping? Something told her that wasn't the case. Rising, went to her window that overlooked the back of the house. She saw him sitting on the stone wall. Somehow, he'd found his way to his favorite spot.

Should she leave him alone?

She wouldn't be able to sleep, knowing he was out

there without anyone to guide him back. He could stumble into the river and drown. She dressed quickly and silently let herself out of the house. The moon was half-full and slipping down in the west, but it gave enough light so that she could make her way to his side.

"Go back to the house, Rebecca. I'm fine. Leave me in peace."

She wasn't sure how he knew she was there, but she wasn't going to be intimidated by his rejection.

"I happen to like watching the river at night." She sat down on the wall.

"I don't need a babysitter. I found my way here, and I can find my way back."

"Fine. Go back to the house and leave me in peace. Do you think you are the only one who is troubled in the small hours the night? You want to see again. I want to hear my husband's voice one more time. I want him to whisper to me that everything will be okay. I want to see him come strolling through the door with a big grin on his face. It isn't fair that he is gone and I am left alone. I know what sorrow is, Samuel Bowman. Explain to me why your loss is so much greater than mine."

"It isn't."

"Each of us must bear the sorrows of this world according to His plan. You have this—I have mine. Sitting here wallowing in pity will not bring my husband back. It will not restore your sight. So we are wasting our time sitting on this cold stone wall when we have comfortable beds. I'm going back to mine. *Guten nacht.*" She stood and started to move away.

"Rebecca?"

She paused. "Yes, Samuel."

"I appreciate all you have done for me."

"I was glad to do it." All she wanted was to comfort him.

"I'm not wallowing in pity out here. I'm searching for a new purpose. I'm listening to His will and trying to learn what He wants me to do."

"I'm sorry I assumed the worst."

"Don't be. I've been wallowing in pity for quite some time."

She sat back down on the wall. "Have you found what you were seeking?"

"Not yet. I feel as if the answer is right in front of me, but I can't make it out."

"I know the feeling."

"Really? You seem like a woman filled with purpose."

"I'm not. I'm struggling, too. I say all the right things, but deep in my heart I'm angry with God and I'm frightened by that anger."

"We are two wounded souls, are we not?"

She smiled, remembering her mother's words. "We are a sad pair, but not beyond hope."

"Will you be going home now? I can feed myself and dress myself. My hands are tender and sore, but I can use them. I don't need a nursemaid."

"I'd like to stay and help through the rest of harvest. Your mother has a heavy workload."

"That would be a kindness. You should go back to bed."

"If you don't mind, I'd like to stay a while longer."

"I don't mind at all."

She remained beside him in contented silence until the moon set, then together they went in.

* * *

Rebecca took a chair in the corner of Dr. Marksman's office. Luke leaned against the wall beside her. She wasn't sure why she was being included in this family meeting with Samuel's physician, but she was eager to hear what he had to say. Not only because Samuel was her patient and her friend, but because she cared deeply about him. Samuel chose to remain in the waiting room.

Dr. Marksman took a seat behind his desk and leaned his elbows on the cluttered surface. The rest of the family sat in a semicircle around him. The doctor folded his hands. "I'm sorry to interrupt your work. I know the timing of harvest is critical. I won't keep you long, but I felt strongly that I needed to have this conversation with Samuel's entire family."

"Have you bad news for us? Is his blindness permanent?" Isaac's tense tone echoed Rebecca's feelings.

Dr. Marksman sat back and drummed the fingers of one hand on his desk. "Samuel's burns are healing well, but I have another concern that I wanted to discuss with you. The damage to Samuel's eyes was minimal."

"Blindness is not a minimal thing," Anna said with a huff.

Dr. Marksman gave her a sympathetic smile. "I don't mean to trivialize his condition, but the physical damage to his eyes isn't severe enough to cause the ongoing problem with his sight."

Isaac tipped his head to one side. "I don't understand what you're saying."

Luke crossed his arms over his chest. "He's telling you that Samuel can see."

Everyone turned to glare at Luke. His mother shook

her head. "Samuel would not pretend such a thing if it were not true. You are calling your brother a liar."

Luke shrugged. "I was with him in the barn yesterday. Oscar reached out to bite, as we all know he can. Samuel blocked him with his elbow. I saw him do it."

Rebecca glanced from face to face. No one believed Luke. She wasn't sure that she believed him, either. "It could have been a coincidence," she offered.

"It looked like a deliberate move to me. That's all I'm saying. A few minutes later he would've fallen over a bucket in front of him if I hadn't guided him around it, but I'm sure he saw the horse was going to bite and he checked him."

Noah sprang to his feet, outrage shining in his eyes. "What reason would Samuel have for pretending to be blind?"

"I don't believe he is pretending," Dr. Marksman said, pulling everyone's attention back to him.

Noah sank onto his chair again. The doctor reached for a book and opened it. "Samuel is suffering from something that used to be called hysterical blindness. Medical professionals now call it a 'conversion disorder,' a condition that causes the patient to show psychological or mental stress in a physical manner. To be honest, I've never treated anyone with this disorder. There is a long list of causes, but most of them point to a type of anxiety or psychological trauma that triggers temporary blindness. Samuel's eyes can see, but emotional turmoil has caused him to block off visual impulses from his eyes to his brain. He isn't doing this on purpose. He is truly blind, but the reason isn't physical."

"Is he aware of this?" Timothy asked.

"I have offered him the same information that I have

given you. He doesn't accept it, and that isn't surprising. He insisted he could see if he wanted to, and he wants to see. A conversion disorder is something a patient can't control."

Isaac scratched his chin whiskers. "Is there a medicine that will help him?"

"There are some treatment options available. Counseling, stress relief, but medicine, no. Since the cause of this disorder is psychological and not medical, I suggested he seek the care of a psychiatrist or psychologist. He refused."

Anna leaned forward. "My son is not crazy. He is blind. You are a poor doctor if you must accuse the patient of not wanting to be well."

"Anna, that is enough." Isaac laid a hand on her arm and she fell silent. He looked at Dr. Marksman. "Will our son recover?"

"There is a good chance his vision will return in time. How much time…that I can't say. I'm hopeful. He has a strong faith and a strong family to help him get through this. Telling him to get over it won't help. Telling him it's all in his head can make it worse. Right now, he has little to dwell on except the horror of what happened. It's still fresh in his memory. As that fades, I believe his vision will return. Slowly or all at once, but there is a slim chance he will never recover his sight. That is up to God."

Rebecca was darning socks for Anna on the porch when Isaac came out of the house the following evening after supper. He took a seat beside her on the small bench. "How is Samuel?"

"Subdued. He's taking a walk along the pasture fence. He uses a long stick to feel his way."

"What do you make of what the doctor told us?"

"I'm not sure what to think. I was happy when he said he believes Samuel will recover in time, but when he admitted he had never seen a case like Samuel's, I did wonder if he knew what he was talking about."

"The thought crossed my mind, as well."

"Samuel is a strong man, but I know he is deeply worried."

"Worried about what?"

Rebecca laid her bowl aside and half turned to face Isaac. "He's worried about the family breaking apart. When I asked him what he meant, he said it was his responsibility to keep his brothers together and he has failed."

Isaac leaned back and stretched his long legs out in front of him crossing them at the ankles. "He has always felt that it is up to him to keep his brothers close even when I tell him young men must go their own way. When Luke left, in some ways it was harder on Samuel than all the rest of us."

"Why do you say that?"

"Samuel was about ten years old when his mother became deathly ill. Anna thought she was dying. I did, too. I had to rush her to the doctor. It was winter. I chose my fastest horse and the small sleigh in order to get Anna to the doctor as quickly as I could. There wasn't room for all the children so I left Samuel in charge. Anna told him he was responsible for all his brothers until I returned. She was barely conscious when I carried her out to the sleigh, but she took Samuel's hand and made him promise to look after the others. I could see in his face how scared he was. I was scared, too."

"We all look after our brothers and sisters. I was always given the task of keeping track of my siblings."

"As was I, but the snow was deep that year, and a big storm moved in. I got my wife to the doctor. An ambulance took us to the hospital, but the roads were soon closed and I couldn't get back. I was worried half out of my mind about Anna and about the boys. During the next three days, Samuel took care of everyone. He did the chores, fed the stock, brought in firewood—he did a man's work and he kept his brothers safe and sound. It couldn't have been easy. Noah was only two. Luke told me later that Noah cried for his mother all the time and Samuel had to carry him around to comfort him. Ever since that time, Samuel has had a profound sense of responsibility toward his brothers."

"Why does he feel he has let them down now?"

"Our farm is a small one. It was enough for Anna and me when the boys were small. But they are grown now and will soon have wives and children. Noah is the youngest, and his family will take over the farm. My other sons will have to find work. Samuel was sure that our woodworking business could be expanded enough to provide a living for everyone. He had the talent and he had the drive to make it work. His mother and I invested all we had to expand. The explosion set fire to the shop and destroyed everything. It was God's will. I don't blame Samuel, but I know he blames himself."

She looked at Isaac. No one knew Samuel better than his father did. "Do you think he will get well?"

Chapter Ten

A dark blue car turned in at the end of the lane and drove toward the house. Rebecca noticed that Isaac hadn't answered her question. He rose to his feet and stepped to the door. "Anna, they're here."

Rebecca tipped her head to look up at him. "Are we expecting someone?"

"Joshua. I had Luke call him yesterday evening. They made good time."

Anna came bustling out of the house drying her hands on her apron. The blue car stopped just beyond the steps. The back door opened. Joshua got out and waved at his mother. She waved back and raced down the steps. Joshua's stepdaughter, five-year-old Hannah, climbed out of the car and ran to meet her. "*Mammi* Anna, I'm so happy to see you again. Do you have some of those cookies I like?"

Anna lifted Hannah into her arms for a hug. "You've grown an inch. The cookies aren't ready. I thought we could bake them together. What do you think of that idea?"

"It sounds *wunderbarr*. I love baking. *Mamm* lets me help her all the time."

Isaac walked down to clasp his son's hand. "Welcome home. We are glad you are back."

"I should have come sooner. Where is he?" Joshua looked around.

"Taking a walk. Come in. Get settled. There will be time to visit after that. Mary, welcome to our home." He smiled at the young Amish woman who got out and stood beside Joshua.

"It's good to be back, although I wish the circumstances were different." The pretty young bride smiled at Rebecca.

The rest of the Bowman brothers came outside and Joshua was soon the center of backslapping and good-natured teasing.

Anna put Hannah down and turned to Rebecca. "You remember Joshua's bride, Mary, and this bundle of energy is Hannah, the granddaughter I have always wanted. Mary, this is Rebecca Miller. She has been helping me take care of Samuel. Come inside, girls. We have a lot of catching up to do. How are my sisters?"

"They are well and send their love. You can expect a letter telling you all about our visit shortly. Tell me, how is Samuel doing?" Mary asked, looking to Rebecca.

"He has had a rough time of it, but he's doing better. His bandages are off."

"But his vision hasn't returned?"

Rebecca shook her head.

Joshua finished paying the driver of the car after they unloaded the bags. "I see Samuel coming this way. I think I'll go out to meet him."

"I'll come with you," Luke said.

"Me, too," Timothy and Noah said together. All the brothers walked toward the pasture in a subdued group.

Isaac smiled after them. "I reckon I'll take the bags in. Tell me again why I had sons?"

Samuel stumbled when he stepped in a hole. He used the pole he carried to catch himself. Simply walking unaided was a challenge, but he was determined to re-learn his way around the farm. He leaned his head on his hands to catch his breath. He might have chosen to walk too far on his first time out, but he wasn't going to sit in the house and learn to knit.

"What's new, *brudder*?"

Samuel jerked his head up. "Joshua? Is that you?" He held out his hand and his brother gripped it. Samuel winced.

"*Brudder*, you are a sorry sight. Leftover pizza that's been walked on looks better than you do."

Samuel grinned as he touched his face. He had been told it was red and raw-looking with scabbed-over areas and shiny red blotches mixed among patches of peeling skin, but Rebecca never mentioned pizza. "You say the sweetest things, Joshua. What are you doing home? I thought you'd be gone another month at least."

"*Daed* asked me to come back and help out. I shouldn't have left before harvest. We could have waited a few more months to get married. I would have been here to help and things might not have gone so wrong."

"You're here now and that's what counts," Timothy said.

"I'm glad you came home. Now I can stop being the only one catching those itchy, prickly corn bundles. It's your turn," Noah said with glee.

"Married men don't catch," Joshua said. Was he able to keep a straight face?

"They don't? Is that true?" Noah demanded. Everyone laughed.

The brothers fell into step together. Samuel realized he was in the middle. Surrounded, guided and protected by the brothers he thought of as his responsibility. It was a big change.

"What are your plans, Samuel? Do you have any?" Joshua asked.

"I don't. I'm still trying to figure out what I can do. Woodworking is out, that's for sure."

"Why?" Noah asked.

Samuel shook his head. "Because I can't see."

"You don't need to see to sand a cabinet panel or a tabletop. We do that by feel," Timothy said.

"I hadn't thought of that." Those were tasks he could do. His hands were still tender, but with a pair of gloves on, he could hold a sanding block or a sheet of sandpaper.

Luke chuckled but didn't say anything. "What?" Samuel demanded.

"You can still stand around and yell at us to get a move on. I know you have eyes in the back of your head that you've used for that."

All of the boys laughed and Samuel joined in.

"We are going to rebuild the workshop, aren't we?" Joshua asked.

Everyone grew silent. Samuel sighed. "The church is building us a new one next week. It won't be as large and it won't have all the equipment we need, but it will be a start."

"All we need is a place to start," Timothy said with

conviction. "God willing, we'll be doing a booming business in a few years and everyone can come back to work here."

"A few years sounds like a long time without you fellas." Noah's voice trembled slightly. "You might find work close by."

"The hardware store in Dover is hiring," Luke said quietly. "So is the place that makes siding in Beach City."

"Beach City? That's more than two day's buggy ride from here," Noah said in disbelief.

"Most decent-paying jobs are more than two days away," Luke snapped.

"No one has to go anywhere." Noah sounded desperate.

"I have a wife and child to support. We could scrape by living here, but what about the next one of us to marry and the one after that?" Joshua fell silent.

"We've always made do." Noah's tone conveyed how much he wanted to believe it was still possible.

Samuel said, "What about the years when the harvest is lean and we don't have enough food to feed all of us? The sad truth is there isn't enough farmland available to support all the Amish in this church district. We need cottage industries. We need to attract customers. We are five miles off a major road. Few people find us unless they are looking for us."

"We'll get by. God will show us what needs to be done." Noah's conviction struck a chord with Samuel. He wanted to believe that, too.

"We trust God to give us a good harvest, but we still have to hoe the weeds from the garden," Timothy said quietly.

Samuel tried for a lighter tone. "I have to find a way to distinguish between a weed and a radish without being able to see them. Any suggestions?"

"Looks like we have more company," Luke said.

"Who is it?" Samuel asked.

"If I'm not mistaken, it's John Miller. I wonder what he's doing here?"

"He's here to put new shoes on *Mamm's* pony." Had he also come to see Rebecca?

Rebecca was visiting with Mary and being entertained by the antics of Hannah and Samuel's mother as they giggled and chatted while they spooned cookie dough onto baking sheets. The aroma of snickerdoodles and gingersnaps filled the kitchen. Isaac was sitting by the window watching, as well. He turned and looked outside. "We have another visitor."

"Who is it?" Anna asked.

"John Miller. Wonder what he wants?"

Anna slipped a full sheet into the oven. "Samuel had me write and ask him to shoe our pony. He said Noah was too busy to do it."

Rebecca moaned inwardly. She hoped John would shoe the horse and leave without asking for her.

"That's a funny face."

Rebecca opened her eyes to find Hannah watching her. "Did I make a face? It must be because I don't like snickerdoodles."

Hannah's eyes widened. "You don't? That's just weird. Did you know my town got blowed away by a tornado?"

Nodding, Rebecca said, "I heard that. It must have been awful."

"It's getting fixed, but it sure is a mess. Lily's *onkel* said one man's troubles are another man's blessings. He has lots of work now for his horses cause they pull logs to the sawmill. There's busted trees all over the place. Lily is my best friend. We're going to go to school together."

Rebecca would have preferred to continue her conversation with Hannah, but John made an appearance in the doorway. "*Guten owed*, everyone."

Anna wiped the sweat from her brow with the back of her hand. "Good evening to you, too. Won't you come in? We're getting ready to enjoy a few hot-from-the-oven cookies."

"That sounds mighty fine. I may take you up on your offer later. First, I'd like to speak to Rebecca. Her mother sent me with a message."

Rebecca tried not to make that face again. She managed a smile and rose to go outside with John. He led the way to a small swing at the end of the porch and sat down. Rebecca reluctantly did, too.

"Is something wrong with *Mamm*?" she asked quickly.

"Ease your mind. It's nothing like that. I happened to mention I was coming this way and she wanted me to tell you that Katie Chupp stopped in to see if you could help out with the children when her baby is born."

"I'll have to find out when she is due. I'm not sure when I'll be finished here."

"Has the family here been treating you well? I've heard Samuel isn't the best patient. He has a reputation for being a hard taskmaster."

"I've been treated very well." She saw the brothers returning from their walk. She realized Joshua would be a welcome addition to the harvest crew. That meant Mary would be able to help Anna. Would Rebecca have a reason to stay on? Samuel no longer needed her care. His brothers or his mother could do all that she was doing. His dressing changes were minimal. He was out and about. If he needed to see the doctor again, Mary or Anna could drive him. Rebecca wasn't needed anymore.

John stared at her with an odd expression. "What's the matter?"

She shook off a feeling of sadness. "Nothing. I was lost in thought."

"Will you be coming home soon?"

"That's exactly what I was thinking about. I'm not sure how long I'll stay, but I'll come home again on Sunday to see *Mamm*." Rebecca would have her old life back soon. Another family wanted her to help with a new baby. Soon her time with Samuel would become another memory. The thought saddened her.

"Your mother will be happy to hear it. May I drive the two of you to Sunday services again?"

His eyes were so hopeful. She smiled at him. "That would be nice. I'll see you on Sunday."

He nodded, but he didn't look as pleased as she thought he would. "Reckon I should get that pony's new shoes on. I'll see you later, and I'll give your mother your message."

"*Danki*, John. I never told you how much I appreciated all the things you did for me after Walter died. You've been very kind to me."

"It's what the family expects of me. That's all."

She found the statement puzzling, but she smiled, anyway. "Don't forget to get some cookies before you go."

"I won't." He walked down the steps as Samuel and

his brothers reached the house. They called a greeting, and Noah went with John to help with the shoeing.

The rest of his brothers went inside, but Samuel stayed by Rebecca. "Did John bring you news from home?"

"Just that my mother misses me, and I have another job offer."

He frowned. "You can't take it. You are still working for me."

"You don't require much care anymore. You said so yourself."

"My fingers are sore and stiff. They may be infected. What do you think?" He held them out.

Taking each one in turn, she examined them carefully. A few of the peeling areas had small cracks in the new skin underneath. She didn't see any serious redness or weeping. "I have some salve in my bag that will help. Wait here and I'll get it."

She wove her way through the crowd in the kitchen, sampling the cookies and teasing Hannah, and returned with a small jar of burn salve. She stepped out onto the porch and saw Samuel was sitting in the swing. Her heart started thudding heavily when she sat down beside him. Being close to John hadn't produced this effect. She schooled her voice into a casual tone. "Let me see them."

He held his hands toward her. She uncapped the salve jar and began smoothing the cream over his palms. "You can use this several times a day. On your face, too. It will help protect the new skin."

"It tingles."

"That means it's working."

"What's in it?"

"It's my own concoction. Aloe vera gel and a few other things. You should wear soft cotton gloves for a while to keep the dirt out. At night, it will be okay to leave them open to the air."

"You like taking care of people, don't you?"

"I have a talent for it the way you have a talent for carving. God gives each of us unique gifts to use for His glory."

"I *had* a talent for carving."

"You still do. How are your eyes today? Any change?"

"The world is still dark. It's strange, but at night, I think I see glimmers of light, almost like stars, but in the light of day, nothing."

"The doctor said this kind of blindness is almost always temporary. You have to have patience."

"It's hard, but I'm trying. Who has offered you another job?"

"Katie Chupp will need a mother's helper when her baby comes. She has five little girls and two boys already."

"Do you like taking care of *kinder*?"

"I love taking care of children. My adult patients are the hard ones to deal with."

"Have I been hard to deal with?"

She crossed her arms. "Do you really want me to answer that?"

"Maybe not."

"You must be glad to have Joshua home."

"It will make things easier for my parents. I'm grateful for that. I could tell he was upset by the scars on my face. Does it look bad?"

"Most of them will fade. In a year, you won't know you were ever in a fire."

"I'm worried about Joshua's daughter. Will I frighten her?"

So that was why he hadn't gone in with the others. "I'm sure Joshua and Mary have prepared her for how you will look. Just remember that children can say hurtful things without meaning to."

"My brother said I looked like a stepped-on slice of pizza. I'm pretty sure his daughter can't do worse than that."

She chuckled. "Aren't brothers wonderful?"

"Yeah, they are."

She heard the pain in his voice and knew he was still thinking that he had failed them. "Might as well get it over with. Your reward will be a warm snickerdoodle."

"How can I say no to that?"

Rebecca guided him into the kitchen and to a seat at the table. His mother brought him a glass of milk. Hannah was standing by her mother at the stove. She frowned when she saw Samuel and glanced up at Mary.

Mary gave her an encouraging smile. "You remember your father's brother Samuel."

Samuel straightened and turned his head toward them. "We met before the wedding, Hannah. You helped me make a trinket box for your mother. Do you remember that?"

Hannah nodded. Mary leaned to whisper in her daughter's ear. "I remember," Hannah said loudly.

Mary gave her a plate of cookies and a little push in Samuel's direction. Hannah approached him cautiously. She set the plate on the table. "Would you like a cookie?"

"Only if they are snickerdoodles. That's my favorite."

"Mine, too. Rebecca doesn't like them. She makes faces."

Rebecca waited for him to comment, but he didn't.

Samuel groped for the plate. Hannah pushed it under his hand. "How come you can't see?"

"My eyes were injured in an explosion." He bit into a cookie.

"Did it hurt?" Hannah asked in a loud whisper.

"A lot, but it doesn't hurt now. These are good. Did you make them?"

"I helped *Mammi* Anna."

"She's about the best cookie maker in the state."

"My *Mammi* Ada is the best."

He chuckled. "Is that your other grandmother?"

"One of them. Are you going to help us pick apples tomorrow?"

"I reckon I could. You'll have to help me. I won't be able to see them."

"I'll show you where they are. He's not scary, *Onkel* Luke."

Luke, leaning against the wall, slapped a hand over his mouth. Timothy punched his shoulder. "You're so busted."

"It wouldn't be the first time," Samuel said. There was a second of stunned silence, then all the brothers laughed.

Noah slapped his knee. "He's got you there. You've been busted by the police and a *kinder*."

Isaac rose from his seat by the window. "Time for bed. We have a silo to finish filling tomorrow, soybeans to start harvesting and hay to cut. The paper says we can expect a chance of rain all next week."

The gathering broke up. The men left and the women

finished cleaning the kitchen. Rebecca was wiping down the table and counters when Anna said, "You have done him a world of good. I'm sorry I doubted you."

"I'm glad I could help."

"It's good to have my family home again. I consider you part of this family now."

Anna went off to bed leaving Rebecca alone in the dark kitchen. She did feel as if she were a part of this family. More so than any other family she had worked with. It was going to be hard to leave. Much harder than she had ever expected.

Instead of going to bed, she slipped out the back door and walked down to the stone wall. Sitting there, she watched the river flowing by. The currents and eddies were marked by ripples, but the true power of the river lay beneath the surface. Like the waters in front of her, her emotions seemed quiet and sedate, but there was turmoil underneath and Samuel was the reason. Her growing attraction to him frightened her. She knew what it was to love and to lose that love, and she never wanted to be in that position again, but Samuel was pulling her toward that very cliff.

Was it possible to turn her feelings back to those of friendship? She had to try.

"A penny for your thoughts."

To her surprise, Luke came out of the shadows beneath the covered bridge. "I'm afraid they're not worth a penny."

"Does that mean you will give them away for free?"

"I was thinking about how hard it will be to leave here."

"That's funny. I'm always thinking about how easy it would be."

She crossed her arms. "You do not like living Amish?"

"I don't have anything against it, just doesn't seem to suit me." He picked up a pebble from the shore and tossed it into the water. The ripple was quickly swept downstream and disappeared under the bridge.

"What does suit you?"

He continued to gaze out at the water. "A fast car. A loud radio. Video games. They suit me."

Tipping her head slightly, she studied his back. "I thought you had more substance than that. They seem like trivial things, not something that could pull a man away from God and from his family."

He glanced at her over his shoulder. "Have you ever ridden in a really fast car?"

"Would it surprise you to know that I have driven a fast car?"

"Don't tell me that pious Rebecca Miller had a wild *rumspringa*?"

"Not as wild as yours from what I've heard, but I left for a while."

He walked to within a few feet of her. "I get what brings kids back. But what keeps them here?"

"First tell me what brings them back?"

"Loneliness. They find they can't fit in. They are square pegs in round holes. The only place where they feel normal is the place they most wanted to leave."

"You didn't mention love."

He shoved his hands in his pockets and walked to the water's edge. "You're right. Love does bring them back because they can't stand being alone."

"So you have answered your own question. Those of us who return and stay, do so because we feel loved.

Loved by God, loved by our families and loved by ourselves. For if you do not love yourself, the world is a very dark place."

He threw another rock in the water. "Yes, it is."

"*Guten nacht*, Luke."

"You're good for him. I hope he sees that."

Rebecca had no reply for him. She simply walked back to the house.

After a long minute, Luke spoke. "Do you see it, *brudder*? Or are you really that blind?"

Samuel came out from beneath the bridge using a long stick to feel his way across the grass to the wall. When he reached it, he sat down. "You should mind your own business."

Luke gave a bark of laughter. "I might make a play for her if you don't. I think she could hold a man's interest for a lifetime."

For once, Samuel knew Luke was right. A lifetime with Rebecca by his side was an image that had cemented itself in his mind and wouldn't fade. Would it be possible or was he only torturing himself?

Luke came to Samuel's side. "Do you think you can make it back to the house?"

"The headache is gone. I'm not dizzy. There's nothing left in my stomach. I think I can. Thanks for your help."

"I don't understand why you didn't have your nurse take care of you."

Samuel rose to his feet, glad to find the dizziness didn't return. "I didn't want to frighten her. If it happens again, I will tell her. Tonight, I'm glad you were the one who stumbled over me. Do you think you can take me back to the house now?"

"Sure, but you should tell Rebecca this happened."

The flash of light Samuel saw when he looked out over the river tonight had produced a blinding headache. The pain dropped him to his knees. For a second, he thought he'd been struck by lightning only there wasn't any sound.

If Luke hadn't come along, Rebecca would've found Samuel sick and rolling on the ground in agony. He was glad she hadn't seen him in that condition.

When Luke said Rebecca was coming, Samuel begged him to stall her until he had a chance to recover. His brother managed to do that, but Samuel knew Luke didn't feel right about deceiving Rebecca.

Samuel didn't, either. He didn't know what the flash of light meant, but it didn't feel like a good thing.

Chapter Eleven

"Something isn't right with Samuel."

Rebecca couldn't put her finger on what was wrong, but he seemed different. Withdrawn somehow. It worried her.

"He looks fine to me," Mary said.

They were all walking toward the small apple orchard a few hundred yards from the house early the next morning.

Samuel held Hannah's hand and let the child lead him. Hannah was excited to pick apples and chatted happily with her grandmother and him. Rebecca walked a few paces behind with Mary.

"Hannah seems quite taken with Samuel," Mary observed.

"He was worried that he would frighten her."

"Joshua and I spent quite a bit of time making sure she understood what had happened to him."

"She's handling it very well."

Mary smiled. "She's strong and she has a wonderful kind heart. How much longer will you be staying? Joshua mentioned that his father hired you to take care of Samuel after his injury. He doesn't appear to need a nurse anymore."

They reached the orchard and Rebecca watched Hannah help Samuel fill his basket with fruit by telling him to reach higher or lower. At one point, he lifted her to his shoulders and let her pick the high ones and hand them down.

Rebecca began filling her basket with the red ripe fruit. "I expected to be sent home when you arrived, but no one has mentioned that. I will have to leave soon or risk losing my next position."

"You have an unusual occupation for an Amish woman."

"I came into it naturally. My husband was ill for many months before he passed away. A friend asked me to be her mother's helper when her baby was born and it was such a joy to take care of a new life. After that, the Lord supplied me with a steady stream of people in need of care."

"My adoptive mother is a nurse. She says it is more than a profession—it is her calling."

"I feel the same way. There are times when I wish I had more education. I may speak to the bishop about that possibility. I know there are some Amish churches that have made exceptions to allow women to be trained as nurses' aides and LPNs." Rebecca finished filling one basket and started on another.

"It's funny that you should mention that. My mother is hoping to help train some of our young women to work at a new clinic being built in Hope Springs. It's a clinic for special needs children. We have a fair number of children with genetic disorders in our district. My mother was raised Amish but chose not to join the church. She speaks Pennsylvania Dutch and that makes it easy for worried Amish families to trust her. She knows how important it is for health care workers to understand and respect the Amish ways."

"That is so true. Our ways are different from the *Englisch.*"

"If you can get permission and would be interested in training with her, I'd be happy to introduce you. We called and told them we were coming back before we left Illinois. She and my father will be coming for a visit soon. I'd like to think they want to see me, but I know it's Hannah that they miss."

"That is an intriguing offer. I will have to give it some thought." Formal training? It was something she had only dreamed about.

"*Mamm,* come see this apple. It's all flat on one side. Isn't it funny?" Hannah came running with her unusual find.

Mary and Rebecca admired it. Hannah took her mother's hand. "Help me find another one."

The two of them went around the next tree. Seeing that Samuel had been left alone, Rebecca moved up to join him. "You have been deserted for an odd-shaped apple."

He smiled slightly, but didn't comment as he gingerly searched the spreading branches of the tree for more fruit.

"Samuel, are you feeling okay?"

His hands stilled. "Why do you ask?"

"You seemed quieter than normal. Is everything all right?"

"I have a bit of a headache. Sorry if I'm putting a damper on the outing."

"You aren't. Hannah is having a good time picking apples, and Anna is having a good time watching her."

Hearing her name, his mother came over to join them. "That Hannah is the sweetest child. After all my sons, I finally have a little girl in the house. I will hate it when they leave."

Samuel scowled. "Who said anything about them leaving?"

"Joshua told us this morning that he is going back to work construction in Hope Springs after the harvest is finished. I know they will come to visit when they can, but I had hoped they would settle here."

"There's no work for him around here, *Mamm*. You know that."

"He must get work where he can, I understand. I just wanted my sons and grandchildren closer."

"I'm sorry I couldn't do that for you," he said quietly.

"It was *Gott's* will. I think we have enough apples for this morning. Let's take them back to the house and start cooking."

Anna called to Mary and Hannah, and the three of them made their way out of the orchard.

"You can't take the blame, Samuel. It was an accident. Accidents happen."

"I know that."

"But you still blame yourself."

"It gives me something to do in the evenings since I can't read a book." He pulled off his dark glasses and rubbed his forehead.

"Is your headache worse?"

"A little."

"Perhaps I should take you to see the doctor."

He settled his glasses back on. "I'm done with doctors for a while, but I am going to need your help getting out of this orchard."

"It will be my pleasure." Rebecca took his arm and led him back to the house, but she couldn't shake the feeling that something was wrong. He was hiding something.

Samuel was sitting on the swing when he heard his mother laugh. He glanced toward the kitchen window and the white curtains fluttering in the breeze. Pain shot through his skull and sweat broke out on his body as he doubled over. Grasping his head with both hands, he held on, enduring the agony until it vanished as rapidly as it came on. At least this time he hadn't been sick. He leaned back in the porch swing and drew a deep breath.

"Another one?" Luke asked. Samuel hadn't heard him approach.

"Yeah."

"You should tell Rebecca."

"This one wasn't as bad."

"It looked bad to me. I thought you were going to fall out of the swing. I'm going to call your doctor."

"Don't."

"Pretend for a minute that it was Noah bending over and grabbing his head. Imagine he's white as a sheet only a few weeks after he went flying through the side of a building following an explosion."

"I flew out an open door, not through the side of the building."

"Good point and that may have saved your life. Back to my story. I say, Noah, I'm going to call your doctor. This head pain isn't right. Now you say?"

"If it was Noah, I'd tell you to call the doctor. I don't need one."

"Because your head is harder than his is or because you think you are less valuable to this family?"

"Fine. Call the doctor, but don't tell Rebecca. I don't want her to worry."

"Good old Luke is the only one who gets to worry. Thanks for that."

"Aren't you supposed to be working somewhere? What do you want?"

"Rebecca asked me to bring these up here and give them to you." He set a box on the swing beside Samuel.

"What is it?"

"A box Rebecca found in the gift shop. They're toys that Timothy cut out before the fire but didn't have time to finish."

Samuel frowned. "What does she want me to do with them?"

Luke took Samuel's hand and laid a sanding block in it. "I think she wants you to finish them. I'm on my way to bale hay with Timothy. I'll call the doctor from the community phone booth."

Leaning back, Samuel folded his arms over his chest. "Why don't you use the cell phone you keep tucked in your boot?"

"Rebecca squealed on me? I don't believe it."

"I heard the low battery alarm beeping while you were washing up last night."

"Oh. I only use it for emergencies."

"I don't care. You aren't a baptized member of our church so you aren't breaking any rules, but don't let *Mamm* find out. Where is Rebecca?" He hadn't seen her all morning. The day seemed incomplete until she was giving him grief about something.

"She's coming this way. I'd better get going."

"Bless you for carrying that box up here, Luke. Samuel, Hannah would like to see how we make our wooden toys. I told her you could show her how it's done. I put a pair of gloves in the box for you to use. The sandpaper will be too rough on your skin. I must get back to the orchard and fetch Anna another half bushel of Red Delicious. Have fun."

He heard her footsteps fade away, and then he heard a tiny sigh from beside him. He hid a grin. "Did you really want to know how these are made or is Rebecca just trying to entertain me?"

He felt Hannah crawl onto the swing beside him. "She's trying to keep you busy so you don't mope."

"She said I mope?"

"Yup."

"She's bossy."

"Yup."

"Which toy do you want to make?"

"Do you have a dog? I miss mine. Her name is Bella, and she lives with *Mammi* Ada."

"You'll have to look and see if there is a dog shape in the box."

"I found one. Now what?"

"We use our sandpaper to rub away the rough wooden edges and make the wood smooth so it looks more like the animal it needs to be."

He heard her start working and before long, he was engrossed in the task of improving a wooden horse and showing Hannah how to do the same with her dog.

* * *

Rebecca glanced out the open window to check on Samuel and Hannah a half hour later. They were both working away. She heard them talking but she couldn't make out what they were saying. Occasionally, she heard Samuel's deep laugh. She loved that sound.

"How are they getting along?" Mary asked as she mashed cooked apples through a strainer.

"Hannah is fine company for anyone."

"It was a good idea."

"I know he would rather be in the fields with the men, or in his workshop, but this is as close to wood-working as he can do at the moment."

"I understand the workshop is being rebuilt soon. Joshua is excited for me to meet all the neighbors and the family members. I know he wishes we could stay here, but I'm happy we are going back to Hope Springs. That reminds me, I finished the letter to my adoptive mother this morning and I told her about your interest in furthering your education. Hopefully, I will have an answer soon and I can tell you when she is coming to visit."

"What is this about more education?" Samuel stood in the doorway. Rebecca hadn't heard him come in. She bit her lower lip, unsure of how he would react. Amish children only went to school until the eighth grade. Additional education was forbidden. The only way a student could go on was to refrain from joining the church.

"Mary's adoptive mother is an *Englisch* nurse. She is looking for Amish women who want to become lay nurses at a clinic for special needs children. She has obtained permission from several of the bishops in the area to train the women. Isn't that a wonderful idea?"

He crossed to the refrigerator and opened it. Pulling out a soda, he popped the top and took a drink. "Is this something you want to do, Rebecca?"

"I'm certainly interested in learning more about it."

He nodded but didn't make another comment. Hannah came in with two wooden toys in her hand. One was clearly a trotting horse; the other, Rebecca wasn't sure what it was.

Hannah carried it to her mother. "See? It looks just like Bella?"

Mary held the toy up and struggled to keep a straight face. "It does look a lot like Bella. You did a great job. Are you finished?"

"Yup. Can I help you now?"

"You can. Bring a chair over here and stand beside me. I'll show you how to make applesauce. Do you want to make plain or cinnamon?"

"Cinnamon."

Samuel went to the broom closet and pulled out his mother's broom. When he went outside, Rebecca followed him. He brushed the sawdust and wood shavings off the swing and then began to sweep the floor. She watched him for a moment.

"Am I missing a lot?"

"*Nee*, you are doing a fine job. Are you upset to learn I wish to further my education?"

"Surprised, but not upset. I see that what you do is important and that you wish to do it well."

"Then why were you surprised?"

"I assumed that you would wish to marry rather than remain single."

"I had considered marrying again so that I might know the joy of my own children, but I don't know if it would be fair to bring *kinder* into a marriage not blessed with a deep love between the parents."

"I understand why you'd feel that way, but respect and friendship can grow into love over time. My mother tells me it's true."

"She told me the same thing. Is your headache better?"

He touched his forehead. "It is. Don't worry about me."

"Are you trying to tell me how to do my job?" She struggled unsuccessfully to keep from smiling.

He held up one hand. "*Nee, nee,* I would not dare. I never know if you have a glass of water handy or not."

"You grow wiser as well as stronger, Samuel. I'm pleased with your progress." She went back in the house with the sound of his laughter raising her spirits.

The next day, Rebecca and Samuel were left at home when all the rest of the family went out to gather hay. Even Hannah was allowed to go along and help. The forecast for pending rain forced Isaac to put everyone to work in the fields. The apples could wait.

Rebecca felt guilty about not helping, but she was still worried about Samuel. She often saw him rubbing his forehead or knuckling his eyes as if they burned. Anytime she asked, he denied having a problem. With everyone gone, she was looking forward to a quiet afternoon of reading to him.

That hope evaporated before she had time to enjoy it. The sound of a horse and buggy pulling up outside drew her to the window. Her heart fell.

"Who is it?" Samuel asked, laying aside his work. He was adding a carved mane and tail to another toy horse with a small penknife.

"It's John Miller."

"No one mentioned that we had more work for him. I wonder what he wants?" Samuel started to rise, but Rebecca forestalled him.

"I'll go see."

She went into the kitchen and opened the door. "Good afternoon, John. What brings you out this way?"

He pulled his hat from his head and bowed slightly. "I thought I would see how Samuel is getting along and perhaps have a private word with you."

That didn't sound good. "Do come in. Samuel is in the other room. I'm sure he will be glad of your company. Everyone else is working in the hay fields."

"A wise move. The paper says it will rain." He smiled tentatively, stepped inside and stood in front of her. He turned his hat around in his hand several times, and then seemed to realize what he was doing. Abruptly, he hung it on one of the pegs beside the door.

She led the way to the living room and he took a seat on the sofa. He looked so ill at ease that she worried he had bad news to share. He ran a finger around his collar. "It's a warm day for this time of year."

"Would you like to sit outside?" Samuel asked. "The breeze off the river is cooling."

John popped up. "That would be fine."

"Why don't you two go out on the back porch and I'll fix some refreshments for you."

John shot out the door like a startled rabbit. What was going on?

* * *

Samuel settled on a picnic table bench against the back wall of the house. There was a good breeze, and it was cooler coming off the river. John paced across the porch and back several times.

"Is something troubling you, John?"

"*Nee*, I'm fine. Why do you ask?" He sounded as nervous as a new preacher on his first Sunday.

"You seem restless today."

"I reckon there's no disguising it. I'm nervous as can be. This is a big step for me, but it's the right one I'm sure."

"What is this big step, and how does it involve me?"

"Not you. *Nee*. I've come to ask for Rebecca's hand in marriage. I know these things aren't usually spoken of, but since she is living here, I see no reason to keep it a secret. We are not teenagers sneaking around at night during our *rumspringa*. We've both been wed before."

John's announcement hit Samuel like a fist to the stomach. Was Rebecca interested in John? She had loved Walter. Who better to take his place than his own brother? There wouldn't be any objections from the church."

"I didn't know that you and Rebecca had been courting?"

"We've seen a lot of each other since my brother died. She is well aware of my feelings. I have been led to believe that she returns them."

"Then you are a blessed man. Rebecca is a wonderful woman." Wonderful and about to fall out of Samuel's reach forever. He cared for Rebecca, but until this moment, he hadn't examined those feelings close enough to realize that he was falling in love with her.

Should he have spoken? Would his blindness matter to her? It wouldn't—he knew that. Not if she loved him. But it mattered to him. John was a good, strong man. He was the better choice for her, but Samuel couldn't imagine how he would feel if she wanted John.

She brought out coffee and cinnamon rolls and sat at the small table beside him, but he had no interest in the food. Fortunately, John had little interest in prolonging the visit. He rose and said, "It was nice talking to you, Samuel. I hope you continue to mend. I'll be back for the workshop raising next week. Rebecca, could you walk me out?"

"Of course."

She sounded puzzled, not like a woman who was eager to hear what the man had to say to her.

Standing, Samuel held out his hand, and John shook it before leaving. Would Rebecca refuse him? Samuel prayed she would, and then he prayed to be forgiven for such a thought.

A headache sprang full-blown behind his eyes. He pulled off his dark glasses and dropped them as he pressed the heels of his hands to his brow to stem the pain. It didn't work. He tipped his head back and opened his eyes. Blue sky and white clouds arched over him. A second later, intense pain dropped him to his knees and he fell forward.

Rebecca walked with John to his buggy. He didn't get in. Instead, he turned around and surprised her by taking her hand. She tried to pull away, but he held on. "Would you like to go for a buggy ride with me?" he asked with a stiff grin.

"That's very nice of you, but I must stay here with

Samuel. No one else is at home." She pulled at her hand again. He finally released her.

"I reckon there's no need for that romantic stuff. I'll say what I have to say, and you can give me your answer." He pulled off his hat and clapped it to his chest.

A sinking feeling settled in her midsection.

"Rebecca Miller, would you do me the honor of becoming my wife?"

She folded her hands below her chin and pressed them together tightly. "This is rather sudden, John."

"No point in beating around the bush. We rub along well together. You'll not want for anything as my wife. God willing, we will have many children to give us comfort in our old age."

With absolute clarity, she saw what her answer had to be. "I like you John, but not enough to marry you. You are fine man, and you deserve a woman who loves you for who you are."

He frowned. "You don't want to marry me?"

She hated hurting his feelings. "I'm sorry. I don't."

He sighed heavily, and then slowly smiled. "Well, that is a relief."

Growing more confused by the moment, she raised both eyebrows. "It is a relief that I won't marry you?"

"It is. My folks are all for it. They have been pushing me for close to six months to wed you. I said yes so they would leave me alone. To think what I put up with when all I had to do was get the right answer from you."

It wasn't very flattering, but she was relieved she'd given him the answer he wanted. "I hope we can still be friends."

"No problem with that. That's all I ever wanted to be. You were Walter's girl."

"And you are his brother. You will always be dear to me."

"I loved my Katie Ann, and I haven't met a woman who could replace her in my heart. I know my folks wanted me and you to be happy together, but this sure wasn't the way."

"Apparently not."

He slapped his hat on his head. "Good day to you. Is it okay if I still take you and your mother to church on Sundays?"

"Of course." How was her mother going to take this news?

"Much obliged. It doesn't feel right traveling to church alone. I'll pick you up at seven sharp tomorrow. The meeting is at Verna Yoder's place."

"You're welcome to stay for supper afterward, too. Anytime."

"*Danki*. That's real nice. I'm glad we had this talk."

He drove away, and it was as if a heavy blanket had been lifted off Rebecca. Shaking her head at the oddity of the whole conversation, she walked through the house headed for the back porch. She pushed open the door. Samuel lay crumpled in a heap beside the table.

Chapter Twelve

Something cold and wet covered his face.

Samuel reached up to pull it down, but someone stopped him. "Leave it on for a few more minutes."

It was Rebecca trying to boss him around again. He was done with that. He yanked the cloth off and threw it aside. He kept his eyes closed tight. He didn't want a repeat of his earlier experience. "I don't need another few minutes."

Had he seen the sky or had he been dreaming? He was afraid to try again. "Where are my glasses?"

"Right here." She laid them on his chest. Fumbling, he managed to get them on and sit up.

"Samuel what happened?"

"I had a dizzy spell."

"Have they happened before?" She had that tone in her voice. The one she used when she was digging for medical information.

"A few times."

"I knew you were keeping something from me."

"How long was I out?"

"Not more than three minutes after I found you. Do you remember anything that might have triggered this?"

Like finding out another man wanted to marry her? "No. Can I get up off the floor now?"

"I don't know if you can, but you may."

"Don't be funny. It's not working at the moment."

"I'm sorry. You're right. Should I go get your mother or one of your brothers?"

He heaved himself to his feet, a little surprised to find he was quite steady. "I don't think they can do anything you haven't done."

"Samuel, I don't think you are being honest with me." He wasn't even being honest with himself. The concern in her voice was genuine. He had no right to worry her.

"This is the third time it's happened, but it's the first time I blacked out."

"You are going to the doctor straightaway."

"Luke has already made an appointment for me. I see the doctor on Monday."

"I guess that will have to do. How are you feeling now?"

"Foolish."

"I don't know why. Very few people have control over their ability to faint."

What about their ability to fall head over heels for a bossy, caring, infuriating widow?

"You haven't been exactly honest with me, either."

"I don't know what you mean."

"John shared his reason for his visit today."

"He didn't."

"Are you going to keep me in suspense until the *banns* are read in church?"

She slapped the wet towel on the back of his neck. It felt good, actually. "I am not going to marry John or anyone else."

His heart gave a happy leap. "You aren't? You turned him down?"

"John and I will continue to be friends. Nothing more."

Relief made him dizzy all over again. He still had a chance. He might have seen blue sky. He might have imagined it. He needed to know for sure before he spoke about his feelings.

He reached out and she took his hand. "I'm sorry that John wasn't the one for you. You deserve to be happy."

She pulled her hand away. "I am happy, but thank you. We need to tell your family about what happened today."

"Really? You want everyone to know you refused John?"

"Don't be funny. It's not working at the moment."

He wanted to make her laugh. It didn't work, but he thought he detected a smile in her voice. He would settle for that. "I don't want to alarm my family."

"How much more alarmed will they be if they discover you in the same condition I did?"

She had a point. "All right, I agree they should know."

Rebecca remained in the background when Samuel shared a watered-down version of his episode that evening when his family came in from the fields. Only his parents appeared to be shocked. The looks shared between his brothers told her they had already discussed the previous episode Luke had witnessed.

It wasn't until she was home and in her own bed that night that the shock of what happened really hit her. The sight of him sprawled across the porch floor would stay with her for a long time. It had taken an eternity to reach his side and make sure he was still breathing. Images of Walter's illness and death swirled through her mind. She couldn't do it again. She couldn't face the possibility of losing someone she loved.

Of losing Samuel.

She had to admit she was already half in love with him. It wouldn't take much to push her over the edge. The question became what could she do about it.

Leaving her employment there was the first step, but she would still see him at every Sunday service, every picnic, every barn raising and school Christmas program.

Only one viable solution presented itself. She could travel to Hope Springs and begin training with Mary's mother. A clinic for special needs children would be the perfect place to follow her calling, and a good place to forget about Samuel Bowman.

She rose hollow-eyed and exhausted from a sleepless night and got ready for church. Her mother and John arrived promptly at seven. She could tell by the look on her mother's face that John had already spilled the beans.

As she climbed in the buggy, her mother squeezed her arm. "I'm so sorry for pressuring you to marry John. He explained that he felt pressured by his family, too. You made the right choice."

"Danki." The right choice yesterday, for what would her mother's reaction be when she told her about her

new intentions. Rebecca decided to save that conversation until they were alone.

During the service, Rebecca kept a watchful eye on Samuel, but he didn't have any problems. Afterward, she was serving the last half of the meal to the younger members when Timothy approached her.

"Could I have a word with you when you are finished here? I'll be out by the greenhouse."

Puzzled, she nodded and Timothy left. Twenty minutes later, she located him sitting on a bale of straw. "What's going on? Is Samuel worse?"

"He's the same. Two weeks ago, you tried to tell us about a plan you had for our business. Samuel wouldn't listen to you then. I'm listening now. What's your idea?"

"It's going to take more than your family to make my idea work. We are going to need the bishop and elders to support this and agree. Do you think you can arrange a meeting for tomorrow afternoon?"

"I can try, but Samuel has a doctor's appointment. Do you want to wait until he can be there?"

"I don't want it put to him until I'm sure the community is on board."

He took a step back. "What are you planning? The takeover of the *Englisch* government?"

"Honestly, that might be easier."

A meeting was hastily arranged, and Rebecca was able to present her idea to a large group in Isaac's living room. Initially, there wasn't overwhelming support, but eventually she made them see the benefit of what she had planned.

Rebecca finished speaking just as Joshua drove into the yard with Samuel in the buggy.

Anna spoke up quickly. "I don't want Samuel to know what we are doing. If what we have to show Mr. Clark isn't what he wants in his stores, then there's no harm done and Samuel never has to know."

Isaac gave a long thoughtful pause. "You mean well, Anna, but I'm not sure I agree with that. A man must learn to face both hope and disappointment in his life. What do you think, Rebecca?"

"Samuel is stronger than he knows. He can face this. He must. It is his dream that we are tampering with."

"She's right, Anna, and you know it." Isaac glanced around the room. "You raised five strong sons. They are not without their flaws, but they are good men in my eyes. Each and every one of them. Rebecca, step out and ask Samuel to come inside. We are anxious to hear what the doctor had to say."

Samuel had hold of Joshua's arm as they approached the steps. Rebecca couldn't keep silent any longer. "What did he say?"

"That there is nothing physically wrong with my eyes." Samuel's terse tone showed his frustration.

"Your parents have company. They would like to talk to you."

"Who is it?"

"The bishop, your uncles and their wives. Some of your mother's kin."

"A crowd. Did I forget someone's birthday? Is it *Mamm's*?"

"You didn't miss her birthday. They have something they wish to discuss with you. A business venture of sorts."

"Of sorts? What does that mean?"

"Come in and see."

* * *

What was Rebecca up to now?

Samuel paused in the doorway to the kitchen. He could feel the crush of bodies in the room. This was more than a few visitors. "What's going on?"

"Come here, Samuel," his father said. Rebecca took his arm and led him to a seat in the living room.

"Who is here?" Samuel asked, staring straight ahead.

One by one, the visitors announced their names. The bishop spoke last. "We have come with a favor to ask of you."

"Of me? I'm not sure what help I can be to anyone."

"Rebecca has presented an idea and we want your opinion of it," the bishop said.

"Rebecca has?" Samuel turned unerringly toward her. He always seemed to know where she was in a room.

"It was my idea, but I don't know if it has merit," she admitted.

"I'm listening."

His father cleared his throat. Whatever it was, he seemed unsure of how to proceed. He drew a deep breath. "We have talked about rebuilding our workshop for our family, but it seems that we have many more people interested in this venture."

Samuel cocked his head slightly. "I don't understand."

"You had hoped to employ your brothers in the workshop making furniture for an *Englisch* firm, is that so?" It was the bishop.

"I did."

"I have some questions about this plan. Was your goal to make money? Or was it something else? If financial gain was the sole reason for the venture, that is not compatible with our beliefs. I cannot condone those efforts. But, I'm willing to listen to what you have to say."

Samuel struggled to put his fading dream into words. "It was never about making money so that we could grow wealthy. My only hope was to provide a living for my brothers so they would marry and raise families here. We all know there isn't enough farmland for our young people. I have seen Amish carpentry businesses that flourished near towns and employed dozens of workers, but not in a rural area such as ours. The *Englisch* can use their internet to show what we make here all around the world. They could take orders, we would build and ship what we make and the *Englisch* would rarely have to come to our place of business. It seemed like the perfect plan."

"I believe your motives are in the best interest of our church and I think the church elders are in agreement with me. We are hoping you can employ more than just your brothers. We have seven young men who will have to leave this area soon to find work elsewhere. None of us wants to see that happen."

Samuel shook his head. "Bishop, even after we rebuild the shop, it won't be big enough to need so many workers."

"But it could be made larger," Rebecca said.

"With better equipment," Timothy added.

"It could," Samuel admitted. "Any building can be made larger. But what is the point if we don't have a place to sell what we make?"

"You already have a man willing to buy what you make. Mr. Clark," Rebecca said quietly.

Samuel threw up his hands. "*Nee*, I do not. He was

willing to come and look over our inventory. We have none."

"That is not true." His mother spoke for the first time. "I have the wooden bench you made for my birthday last year and the china cabinet in the living room. My niece has the table and chairs you finished for her wedding gift. It was on the wagon and not harmed in the fire."

"I have the Bible stand you made for Walter. It's a remarkable piece. The carving is done in deep relief and the lines of it are beautiful." Rebecca spoke softly.

They all wanted so much to help. How could he make them understand how pointless it was? "I can't very well ask this man to travel to every home in our church district to look at a scattering of furniture."

"You won't have to."

He turned toward Rebecca's voice. There was an undercurrent of excitement in her tone. "What do you mean?"

"On Thursday, every household in this church district and many from the neighboring districts will be here to help with the workshop raising. They'll come in wagons with tools and supplies and they can bring their furniture with them. All we will have to do is assemble it where Mr. Clark can look it over."

She made it sound almost logical. A curl of optimism began to form in his chest. "What if it rains?"

"We'll bring the tents and awnings we use at the farmer's market," someone said from the back of the room. A murmur of assent followed his words.

How could he get their hopes up? What if his work wasn't up to the standards of this unknown man? "What if he decides he doesn't want to purchase furniture from us?"

Someone laid a hand on his shoulder. "Then we shall have a fine new workshop thanks to the generous spirit of our friends and neighbors and we'll have a *goot* time raising it," his father said. "What more could we ask? If this is *Gott's* will, it shall be so."

Samuel wasn't convinced. "Mr. Clark might not even come. He knows what happened here."

"I'll convince him," Timothy said. "I can be very persuasive when I put my mind to it."

Samuel couldn't believe what was happening. He was being given a second chance at fulfilling his dream. Not just for his family, but for other young men in his community who didn't want to leave. If his sight didn't return, he would have to depend on others to carry on the bulk of the work. It was no longer about his skill, but about the skill of those around him.

"All right, but I won't be making furniture for a while, if ever. I want people to bring Father's work and Timothy's work, too, so we can showcase it. I want the table and chairs you made for that *Englisch* family over by Berlin."

"The Rock family?"

"That's the one. It was good work. Your best. See if you can get it here. Luke, you made a chest for the doctor's office. Ask if you can borrow it for a day."

"It wasn't a typical Amish piece," Luke said. He had been sitting quietly at Samuel's side. "All the drawers are different sizes and shapes.

"I know, but it is well crafted and eye-catching. You've all made a number of pieces. Track them down and get them here. It can't be about my work. It has to be about *our* work." Excitement began to build inside Samuel. Where was his mother? "*Mamm*?"

"What, *sohn*?"

She was across the table from him. He reached out his hand and she took it. "This whole thing is going to rest on your shoulders," he said as seriously as he could manage.

"On mine? How?"

"If Mr. Clark comes, you will have to soften him up with your *wunderbarr* cooking. Once he is in a state of lemon meringue bliss, he won't be able to say no to our proposal."

A round of laughter followed his teasing. A flurry of discussion and details followed. It was growing late by the time everyone went home. At last, there was only Luke in the kitchen with him. "Do you know where Rebecca went?" Samuel asked.

"I saw her go out the back door a little while ago. Do you want me to find her?"

"*Nee*, I think I know where she is. I want to thank you, Luke."

"For what?"

"For believing in me even after I failed to believe in you."

"Who said I believe this harebrained scheme will work?"

"You did."

"When?"

"When you sat shoulder to shoulder with me and listened to all my doubts without agreeing with any of them."

"Maybe I was waiting until we were alone."

"We're alone now. Do you think it can be done?"

"Building a workshop? Sure."

"I meant keeping this family together. I meant keeping you here with us."

"You know I'm not fond of living in the dark ages. I like the city lights. Having a business that will support a number of families will keep Timothy and Joshua here. Noah, I'm not so sure about him. I know he's the one who will eventually inherit the place, but he has a bit of wanderlust in his heart."

"As long as there are horses on this farm, Noah will stick around. I'm not worried about him. If you have to go, Luke, I'll understand this time and I won't hold it against you."

"I'll stay until I see how this harebrained scheme plays out. Longer than that? Who knows?"

Samuel reached out to find his brother's shoulder. "God does."

Seated on the low stone wall beside the river, Rebecca watched the sunset behind the covered bridge. The last faint rays of light came through the wooden slats in bands of brightness filled with spiraling dust motes.

"Rebecca?"

She heard his low query behind her. Tempted to remain silent and let him go away, she closed her eyes.

"I know you are here. Please answer me."

"How do you know?" she asked without opening her eyes. She was aware of him, too, even when she couldn't see him.

"I hoped you were." He felt his way along the wall and took a seat beside her. "What does the river look like tonight?"

"It's gray and muddy."

"*Nee*, it isn't."

"If you know, why did you ask?"

"Because I want to know what you see when you look out from here."

She sighed. It was going to be so hard to leave, but going away was for the best. Every time she crossed the bridge in the future, she would think about sitting here and watching the sun go down or seeing the moon cast rippling silver light all the way to the water's edge.

"Take pity on me and tell me what you see."

"I don't pity you, Samuel. In some ways, you are more blessed than most."

"I am blessed, but I miss my old friend the river. How is he?"

"The sun is setting behind the bridge. There is a stream of golden light running toward us from beneath the timbers. Spears of light are shining through the sides of the bridge now. It looks as if the sun is inside it."

"It must make the colors of the trees glow like fire. The reds are redder and the yellow leaves are bright golden in the light. There are dozens of them floating along in the water, turning this way and that."

She glanced at him sharply, wishing he wasn't wearing dark glasses and that she could see his eyes. "Can you see them?"

"*Nee*, but I know what the river looks like this time of year. I remember. Was it truly your idea to gather up my work to show Mr. Clark?"

She pulled on the ribbons of her *kapp*. "I had the idea, but your father and Timothy worked out most of the details."

"I'm afraid what we have to offer won't be what he wants."

"He won't be able to take any of it back with him. Will that make a difference?"

"The time I spoke with him he mentioned that his plan was to photograph the work and build an online and print catalog where people could order similar items but customize them."

"That makes me feel better."

"I wish I could say the same."

She took his hand in hers and held it to her cheek. "Have faith, Samuel. I have faith in you and the gift God has placed in you."

He pulled his hand away. "I no longer have the gift He gave me."

"You do. You just have to find a new way to use it that will glorify God."

The urge to take her in his arms and kiss her was almost more than Samuel could bear. He rose to his feet and took a step away. She was kind and sweet and full of life. Being near her made him think about a future that couldn't be. Not unless he regained his sight. She had already lost one husband. She deserved a whole man. Not John, but someone she could love as she had Walter. He wouldn't ask her to settle for less.

He moved another step away. "I appreciate your confidence, but I'm not sure it's well-placed."

"Tomorrow will be my last day here, Samuel."

He knew it was coming. "You'll be missed."

Did she have any idea what she did to him? He couldn't think clearly when she was so near.

"I've enjoyed my time here. I proved Verna Yoder wrong. You weren't a bad patient."

He smiled because he knew she wanted him to. He blinked back the sting of tears and squeezed his eyes shut.

When he opened them, her face swam into focus. There were tears on her cheeks.

His breath froze in his chest. There wasn't any pain this time. He took in her delicate beauty, her white-blond hair beneath her *kapp*, the small white scar on her chin. He wanted to shout for joy.

He blinked again, and she was gone. Nothing but blackness surrounded him.

For a second, the despair nearly overwhelmed him, but he hung on to one ray of hope. The stars, the blue sky, her face, they were real. His vision was recovering.

Should he tell her?

What if it was a fluke? What if that glimpse was all he ever had of her face?

He would wait to be sure before he mentioned it, but he had hope for the first time in weeks.

The morning of the workshop raising dawned clear and bright. The chance of storms never materialized. Before the sun rose, wagon after wagon began arriving loaded with lumber, ladders, well-wrapped pieces of furniture and entire families from grandparents to new babies. *Englisch* as well as Amish families came to share in the work.

Mary darted forward in excitement when she saw a white SUV turn in. Hannah clapped her hands. "That's Papa Nick and *Mammi* Miriam. I hope they brought Bella." She ran after her mother, and Rebecca watched a happy reunion take place between the child and a big yellow dog.

Buggies and carts continued to come and soon a long line of them bordered the driveway. The corrals were crowded with horses and the lawn was overrun with children, while the men set up long trestle tables and tents and the women brought out mountains of food.

The foundation of the building had been poured the week before and the concrete slab was dry. The ring of hammers filled the air as the walls were assembled. When the first one was ready, Noah brought out a team and hitched them to a rope attached to the top of the wall. At a word from Isaac, he put the team in motion. The animals leaned into the collars as they pulled the wooden structure upright aided by a dozen men leveraging long poles. The poles were then braced into the ground to hold the wall steady until it could be secured. The adjoining wall went up the same way, and by noon, the skeleton of a building was standing where only empty ground had been the week before.

At Samuel's suggestion, the building site had been moved closer to the highway to make deliveries of lumber easier. A gravel parking lot would be added for cars and trucks when the building was complete.

Rebecca stared at the building being finished before her eyes by an army of men swarming over it. Soon the siding would go on and the young boys would be recruited to start painting. Where was their furniture buyer?

Mary came to Rebecca with a tall *Englisch* woman at her side and introduced her as her adoptive mother, Miriam Bradley. Rebecca shook her hand. "I'm pleased to meet you."

"Mary tells me you are interested in working with us in Hope Springs. We'd love to have you."

"Truly?"

"Mary tells me you've done a lot of lay nursing already. I can't guarantee you a job, but I can promise you an interview with our doctors. Just show up."

Glancing toward Samuel handing boards to others from the back of a wagon, Rebecca hesitated. She cared so much for him. The longer she stayed the more her love would grow. She turned to Miriam. "I'll be there as soon as I can get a bus ticket."

"Wonderful."

Rebecca worked beside Anna as they got ready to serve lunch to nearly one hundred people. She tried to keep her mind on her tasks, but she couldn't keep her gaze away from the highway. Where was Mr. Clark? Why wasn't he here yet? Had he found another carpenter to supply his needs?

An *Englisch* fellow with a gourd birdhouse under his arm strolled up to Anna. He was wearing faded jeans and a green plaid shirt with the sleeves rolled up. He had a tool belt on and wore a pair of worn work boots. "Are you the woman I see about buying one of these? I took it off the tree out by the highway, but it didn't feel right to leave the money there. Aren't you afraid someone will steal it?"

Anna smiled at him. "If they do, then they need the money much worse than I do. All the birdhouses have been paid for, and all the money has been there each morning when I check. If you treat people honestly, they will behave honestly."

He handed over several bills. "That is an interesting

philosophy. I'm not sure it's one my stockbroker could live by, but I think you're right."

"Bless you for coming to help my family rebuild."

"It's been my pleasure. I've always wanted to attend an Amish barn raising. This was as close as I could get. It felt great to pound some nails. It's been a while. The craftsmanship going into that simple building is amazing. I think it will be standing long after I'm gone."

"God willing, sir. God willing. Let me fix you a plate of food. You must be hungry after all your work this morning."

"I am. Thank you."

Rebecca looked again toward the road. Samuel stood beside his father at the end of the driveway. Noah and Timothy were patting each other on the back and grinning.

Anna handed the workman a plate piled high with fried chicken, fresh corn on the cob and creamy mashed potatoes. He smiled broadly at the sight. "My cardiologist would have a heart attack just looking at this."

"Hard work deserved *goot* food. I'm Anna Bowman."

He nodded. "I'm James Clark, and you have some fabulous pieces of furniture assembled here, Mrs. Bowman."

Noah came charging through the crowd and skidded to a stop beside his mother. He whispered something in her ear. Anna's eyes brightened at his words. She slapped her hands to her face. "God be praised. Praise His holy name."

Chapter Thirteen

Samuel sat with his family at the kitchen table late that evening. He was bone tired but too excited and happy to head to bed. "Rebecca's plan was a success. Mr. Clark not only liked what he saw in furniture, he liked the layout of the workshop and made some excellent suggestions about tools and equipment that could be purchased at a later date."

"When the contracts are signed, we will have orders for twenty-five pieces worth hundreds of dollars and the promise of more work once the website and online catalog are updated." Timothy sounded happy enough to jump for joy.

"It was a long day, but a *goot* one," Anna said with a deep sigh.

Noah held up his left hand. "My thumb is sore."

Luke laughed. "You are supposed to hit the nail with the hammer, not your thumb."

"Ha, ha. Yours is black-and-blue, too."

"Because some fool stepped on it when I was climbing the ladder."

"Who are you calling a fool?" Timothy demanded.

"Was that you? I could've fallen to my death if I had lost my grip."

Samuel removed his dark glasses and rubbed his eyes. "You couldn't have fallen to your death. You were standing on the ground at the time, and you stuck your hand right where Timothy was coming down."

"How did you know I was standing on the ground?" Luke grumbled.

"Actually, I saw the whole thing."

His brothers chuckled at the joke. Samuel folded his glasses and tucked them in his pocket. "You have some mashed potatoes on your dress, Mother."

"Do I?" She brushed at her chest. "I always end up with something down the front of me."

Noah's eyes grew round. "Do you really see the potatoes, Samuel?"

"What?" Anna stopped cleaning the spot and gazed at her son. "Are you making a joke?"

"I can't see everything. It's like looking through the bottom of a canning jar, but I can see you."

Everyone began talking at once. Anna broke into tears. When the first rush of astonishment died down, Luke waved his hand in front of Samuel's eyes. "How many fingers do you see?"

"Five and they need to be washed."

"When did it come back?" Isaac asked.

"Last night. I was down by the river talking to Rebecca and I saw her face for a second before everything went dark again. Actually, I had seen flashes before, but they were so painful I didn't know what was happening. When I woke up this morning, I could see where the window was, but not much else. On and off throughout the day it would come and go. About seven o'clock, it stopped fading to gray and stayed bright. I've been waiting for it to go away again, but it hasn't. I didn't see the potatoes until just now, *Mamm*."

He wished Rebecca were here to share his joy.

"God is great, and God is good." Isaac declared. "Let us bow our heads and give thanks for the many blessings we have seen today."

Samuel voiced his deepest fear. "I don't know if I'll still be able to see when I wake up tomorrow."

"That bridge cannot be crossed until you reach it, Samuel." Isaac bowed his head and the entire family followed his lead.

The next morning, Samuel reluctantly opened his eyes and focused on the ceiling above him.

"Well?"

He turned his head to the side and saw all four of his brothers seated beside his bed. "Your faces are the scariest things I've ever seen."

They all grinned.

"What's on the agenda for today?" Noah asked. "Harvest is over. The workshop is built but we don't have enough lumber to start anything. I say we go fishing down at the river."

"Seconded." Joshua raised his hand.

Samuel sat up and stretched. He couldn't remember the last time he'd slept so well or felt so strong in the morning. "You guys will have to go without me. I've got something I have to do first."

"He's got to go see Re-bec-ca. I smell a romance." Timothy winked.

Joshua's grin faded. "I'm not sure Rebecca is still here."

Samuel let his arms fall to his sides. "What do you mean?"

"Mary said Rebecca was leaving on the bus today. She's joining Mary's mother at the special needs clinic in Hope Springs."

"She wouldn't go without saying goodbye." Samuel glared at his brothers. "Get out of here. I've got to get dressed."

Packing took less time than her breakfast, and that had only been a cup of coffee.

Rebecca folded her last pair of socks and put them in the suitcase. She owned four work dresses and two good ones. The deep blue one she was wearing at the moment was her Sunday best. She would wear it on the bus. *Kapps*, aprons and assorted articles of clothing went in next.

With each addition to the pile, she grew less and less certain that she was doing the right thing.

How was Samuel today? Was he happy with the success he had achieved? Were his eyes bothering him? Had he had any more spells? Was he taking care of himself or was he ignoring her advice to wear gloves?

Did he miss her the way she missed him?

That was a foolish question.

They were all foolish questions. Samuel wasn't her patient anymore. He was a friend. They would wave when they saw each other on the road. He might speak to her when she served his meal after church, but their lives would drift apart. The closeness they shared would fade. It had to. Unless it did, she was going to be miserable for many, many years.

"Rebecca, do you want me to pack any of your books?" her mother called from downstairs.

Her mother was helping close up the house until they found someone to rent it. She hoped it would be a young couple with children. A home should have children to make it feel loved.

She heard her mother coming up the stairs. Rebecca wiped the tears from her eyes and started folding her handkerchiefs.

"What are you doing?" Samuel's voice froze her in place. Why hadn't her mother warned her he was coming up?

Rebecca couldn't face him. She fought to hold back her tears and keep her voice steady. "I have a new job in Hope Springs. I'm moving there. I'm so excited."

"You don't sound excited."

She cleared her throat. "I am. What are you doing here?"

"I came by to tell you the good news."

"I heard Mr. Clark say he was going to place his orders with you. That's wonderful."

"My vision has come back, Rebecca."

She closed her eyes and pressed her hands to her mouth. "I couldn't be happier for you. That's wonderful. God is good. I told you to have faith."

There was a moment of awkward silence. She almost turned around, but she didn't.

"Do you want to leave?" he asked quietly.

"I'm following my heart's desire."

"What about us?"

She sniffed and pressed the clothes flat in the case. "You're well. You don't need me anymore."

"I reckon it's true enough that I'm well. I can see

almost as good as I used to. My hands are still tender, but I can work if I'm careful."

She began packing her jars of herbs into her satchel. "They will get better, too. Don't forget to rub my salve on them. It will help."

"What potion do you have for my heart, Rebecca?"

She paused but still couldn't turn around. She heard him step closer. The nerves in her skin sprang to life. He was so close that if she leaned back she could rest against his chest as she had done that night by the covered bridge.

"There's nothing wrong with your heart, Samuel."

"But there is, and you are the cause."

"I never meant to hurt you."

"You're hurting me now. I want to spend my life proving how much I care for you. Tell them you've changed your mind. Stay here. Please, don't go.

Oh, how she longed to remain in Bowmans Crossing and be near him. Only it couldn't be. He deserved a woman who could love him without fear. Without dread holding her back as it held Rebecca back now.

She fixed a smile on her face and turned around. "I can't stay. I want to take this job."

He looked stunned. Her fingers itched to caress his face, to ease his pain, but she curled them into a tight ball. His voice wavered when he spoke. "I know I can't replace Walter, and I don't want you to forget him. Do you care for me at all?"

"I'll always hold our friendship dear, but my husband still holds my heart." It wasn't true anymore, but she couldn't admit it.

"I'm sorry I bothered you." Samuel turned away, but

paused with his hand on the doorknob. "I bid you farewell, Rebecca Miller."

"Goodbye, Samuel."

When he closed the door behind him, Rebecca spun around and threw herself onto her bed. The tears she had struggled to hold back broke free, and she sobbed as if her heart were breaking. She was still sobbing when her mother came in a short time later.

"There, there. Don't cry, child." *Mamm* gathered her close and held her until her tears finally ran dry. Rebecca's sobs tapered into occasional hiccups.

Mamm put a hand under Rebecca's chin and lifted her face. "You refused Samuel, didn't you?"

Rebecca sniffed and nodded. "Did he say something?"

"Nothing needed to be said. I could tell from the way the light had left his eyes that you turned him down. I hoped and prayed that you had found love again, Rebecca. I'm rarely mistaken about these things. Do you love Samuel, or has John claimed your heart?"

"I don't love John. I'm sure of that. I'm not sure that I love Samuel, but I think I do."

"Then why send him away?"

"When Walter died I almost died, too. I wanted to lie down on his grave and never get up. I wanted the snow to cover me and numb all my heartbreak. Living alone is better than risking such pain again."

"Nonsense!" Her mother scowled at her.

"What if I accepted Samuel's offer of marriage and I found I didn't love him as I should? How unfair would that be if Walter were always between us? Samuel would grow to hate that. I had a wonderful husband, but he is gone. My calling now is to care for others."

"I understand fear, child. I understand that it is hard to trust that God knows best. Yes, you have suffered a great loss, Rebecca. No one can deny that, but to believe God wants you to spend your life without love is folly. Surely you believe in God's boundless love."

"Of course I do."

"He loves us beyond all understanding."

"What do you want me to say?"

"I hear you saying the right things, but do you truly believe them?"

Did she? Why was it so hard to believe God would bring love back into her life and not whisk it from her?

"Rebecca you have to make a choice. Will you let love or fear rule your heart? You can give your fear over to God, or live a shadow of the life He has planned for you."

"I rejected Samuel. There's nothing more to say."

"Tell me one thing. In all the days you were with Samuel, taking care of him, working to make his business dream a reality, spending time alone with him, how many of those moments did you feel Walter standing between you?"

"Never."

"I thought so. You are the only person standing in the way of your happiness. Stop blaming Walter. Stop hiding behind your fear of loss.

Rebecca closed her eyes. She had made such a mess of things. "What do I do?"

"Find Samuel and tell him what's in your heart. That's all you can do. And pray."

She didn't love him.

Samuel took refuge from his family's prying eyes

on the banks of the river below the covered bridge. He realized as he stared into the water sweeping past that it wasn't the best choice of hideouts. There were too many memories associated with this place.

He remembered the nights when he and Rebecca sat in companionable silence on the stone wall or teased each other with glee. He could almost hear the sound of her laughter in the gurgling water. He could feel the peace she brought him in the warmth of the sun overhead. It was impossible to imagine life without her.

What could he have done differently? What could he have said that would've convinced her of his love? He knew the answers. Rebecca had made her choice and nothing he said or did would change that. He prayed for her happiness even as he knew it would be a long time before he felt joy again.

He stared at the reflection of the bridge in the water. It was like the future he had dreamed of with Rebecca. It was pretty to look at, but a man couldn't cross the river through it.

Movement in the reflection caught his eye. Someone was walking on the bridge. He saw glimpses of a blue dress moving between the slatted sides. It took a second for him to realize the woman had stopped moving. She was staring over the railing at the water below. The current kept her face from coming into focus. It was easy to imagine it was Rebecca looking down at him, because that was what he wanted with his whole heart and soul.

He picked up a stone and threw it in. The ripples distorted everything. When the water settled, the woman was gone. Maybe his eyes were playing tricks on him again.

No, she wasn't gone. He looked closer and then looked up. Rebecca stood staring at him over the railing. His heart thudded so hard that he feared it couldn't keep beating. She was here. She hadn't left.

Why was she here?

"Samuel, I need to speak with you. I'm so sorry. I was afraid, and I hurt you. Can you forgive me?"

He sprang to his feet. "What are you saying? Never mind, I'm coming up."

"No, stay there. I'm coming down." She vanished from his sight and for a moment, he wondered if she had been a hallucination.

He bolted up the bank toward the road just as she started down. He wasn't dreaming. She was real.

The footing on the hillside was treacherous. In her haste, she lost her balance and tumbled forward, straight into him. The impact knocked him backward. He staggered but managed to stay upright.

She was in his arms at last. He had dreamed of this moment. He didn't want to breathe. She gazed up at him with wide startled eyes. The desire to press his lips to hers overrode his better judgment, and he kissed her.

After the briefest hesitation, her lips softened and yielded to his and she was kissing him back. His heart soared and he didn't care if it was beating or not. He could have died from happiness. He never wanted to let her go. The glorious kiss went on until his body demanded air.

He drew back and the rush of passion settled enough for him to make sense of what was happening. "I love you, Rebecca, but I thought you were leaving."

"I couldn't go without telling you that I love you,

too. I'm sorry I turned you away. I won't turn you away again. Ever."

He cupped her cheeks in his hands. "I can't believe that I'm holding you."

"I can't believe that I almost let you slip away."

"You said that you were afraid. Of what? I would never hurt you."

"I was afraid to reach for happiness again. I was afraid it would be taken away and I would be left alone. Then I realized that if I didn't reach for it, for you, I was still going to be alone. I want to share every minute of my life with you for however long God grants us."

He kissed her again and then enfolded her in his embrace and held her tight. Nothing had ever felt as right as this moment. "Thank you for being brave, my love. Thank God for bringing you into my life and giving me the chance to see how wonderful you really are." He kissed the top of her bonnet.

"You are the one who gave me the strength to try." She raised her face to his in a silent invitation and he gladly complied.

Rebecca couldn't believe the joy swelling her heart. He loved her and she loved him, too. She knew Walter was watching from Heaven and smiling on her.

"*Onkel* Luke, look! *Onkel* Samuel is kissing Rebecca!"

She and Samuel looked up to see Hannah leaning over the bridge railing staring at them with startled eyes. A second later, Luke appeared.

He propped his elbows on the wooden rail. "It's about time. I thought I was going to have to hog-tie the two of you together."

Heat rushed to Rebecca's face, and she hid it against Samuel's chest. How embarrassing.

Samuel waved him off. "Go away. I'm busy, as you can see."

Luke didn't move. "Don't mind me. Just pretend I'm not even here."

Rebecca chuckled and glanced up. "Don't you have work to do?"

"Nope. Hannah, do you have work to do?"

The child shook her head. "I don't have a job, *Onkel* Luke. I'm too little. Should we tell *Mamm* and *Daed* about this?"

He took her hand. "We should definitely tell. Come on. Let's go find them."

They vanished from sight and Rebecca pressed her face to Samuel's neck again. He was so strong, and he smelled wonderful. She knew she would never tire of being held by him. "How much time do you think we have?"

"Sixty years or so. Why?" He slipped a finger under her chin and lifted her face.

"I meant until your brothers show up."

"Two or three minutes."

"Then you had better kiss me again, Samuel Bowman, before we are interrupted."

"Have I mentioned that you're bossy?"

She giggled at the memories of their early times together. "A time or two."

"Have I told you how much I love you?"

His voice, so deep with emotion, sent a thrill of joy pouring over her. "Not nearly enough."

"I love you, Rebecca Miller. God has blessed me

beyond my wildest dreams. I think I'm going to have to marry you."

"You come up with the best ideas." She cupped his cheek with her hand. His scars were fading, but he would always carry a reminder of the events that brought them together.

"Will you?" he asked.

"Will I what?"

"Don't tease me. Will you marry me?"

"Is that the only way I'll get another kiss?"

"If you say yes, you'll get a lifetime of kisses thrown in for free."

"Then how can I refuse such a deal?"

His eyes grew serious and he pulled back a little. "Are you sure? I don't want you to regret this decision. My sight may fail again. Our business may not prosper as I hope. I want you to be happy. I don't want to tie you to a failure."

"Are you trying to talk me out of it now?"

"Maybe. Holding you feels too good to be true."

"Shall I toss some water on you to prove I'm really here?"

"You would, wouldn't you? What was I thinking to propose beside a river?"

She smiled as she placed both hands on his cheeks. "I know you are afraid of losing your sight. I'm afraid of losing you. How can we honor God in our lives if we live in fear of what may happen to us? I love you. God brought me love when I thought I could never feel it again. If today is the only day I'm given to show you how much I love you, then it will be enough."

He kissed her forehead and then her eyes, and she rejoiced in the tender touch of his lips against her skin.

He pulled her tight against his chest and whispered, "I will never tire of your wisdom, Rebecca."

"And I will never tire of being in your arms. I'm going to trust God to make our lives joyful. I'm going to trust that he will give us children to love and years to work together side by side. I know He is going to give us obstacles to overcome and trials to endure, but I will do my best to make you a good wife if you will have me."

"I can't ask for more."

"Then we have a deal?"

"We do." He kissed her soundly to seal the bargain. Wrapped up in each other's arms, they didn't notice two more witnesses standing on the back porch of the house.

Isaac, a twinkle in his eye, pulled his wife close and gave her a peck on the cheek. "Two sons matched and only three more to go. The Bowman bachelors are falling fast."

Epilogue

The last Thursday in November

"So you're really going to go through with this?"

Samuel chose to ignore Luke's question and raised his chin. "Button this stubborn button for me and then button your lip."

Luke chuckled. "I'm not the fellow with shaky hands. All I'm saying is that I have a fast horse and buggy outside if you need one."

Run away from a life with Rebecca as his wife?

Never.

As quickly as they had come on, Samuel's unexpected jitters fled. He drew a deep breath and flicked Luke's wide-rimmed black hat off his head. "The only need I have for a fast horse is to carry me to my wedding that much quicker."

Luke caught his hat before it hit the floor and settled it on again. "Then I'm at your service, *brudder*. Let's hope the bride feels the same."

Samuel pulled his new black coat on over his white shirt and quickly tied his black bow tie. "She does. I've no cause to doubt her. God chose us to love and care for each other."

He picked up a small packet from his bedside table and tucked it inside his vest, then he led the way downstairs and out onto the porch where Timothy, Noah and Joshua waiting. They were all dressed alike in dark trousers, white shirts, dark coats and wide-rimmed black hats. They all sported the same foolish grin Samuel knew he was wearing.

Joshua stepped forward to brush a speck of dust from Samuel's shoulder. "Did Luke give you his 'I've got a fast horse' speech?"

"He did."

Luke shook his head as he walked past and paused at the top of the steps with his thumbs hooked under his suspenders. "He gave me the same answer you did, Joshua. I don't get it. I can't imagine a woman who would make me want to settle down and live my entire life in Bowmans Crossing."

Samuel shared a smile with his married younger brother. "I pray I live to see the day he does find her."

Noah pushed Luke off the step. "I pray for the poor woman who thinks she wants a lazy good-for-nothing like you."

Luke whirled around with his hands clenched into fists, but there wasn't any malice in his eyes, only a good-natured invitation to start some fun. The entire family had been up since four-thirty getting ready for the wedding day. The cows had been milked, the stock had been fed and the buggy had been washed. The men were all dressed in their Sunday best. Samuel's parents had left hours ago to help with the wedding feast preparations at Rebecca's home, where the wedding would take place. It was almost seven-thirty and time to be on their way.

Samuel stepped between his brothers and put a hand on each one's chest. "Get me to my wedding before you get into a wrestling match. Please."

Timothy had already climbed in the waiting buggy and held the reins. "If Rebecca wants to marry into this family, she's one brave woman."

His heart pounding with happiness, Samuel hopped in beside Timothy, leaving the others to jostle for position in the back. "*Ja*, Rebecca is that and so much more than I deserve. God has truly blessed me."

"I'm such a coward." Rebecca rubbed her hands together to warm her freezing fingers. She cast imploring glances at her four *newehockers*—her side-sitters, the women who would be her attendants and sit at her side during the ceremony and afterward at the wedding feast. They were all dressed as Rebecca was in identical pale blue dresses with white capes and aprons. Only Rebecca, as the bride, wore a black *kapp*. She would trade it for a white one later in the day.

Mary, Joshua's wife, stepped forward and took Rebecca's hands in hers. "You are not a coward. Every bride has an attack of nerves. It's only natural. Do you love Samuel?"

"Of course I love him, but what if I'm not the best wife for him? I wasn't always the best wife to Walter. I should have been a better helpmate. I should have seen what was wrong sooner. I don't want to make a mess of Samuel's life. He has struggled so much already."

Rebecca's dear cousin Emma Swartzentruber sat primly on the edge of Rebecca's bed. A smile twitched at the corner of her mouth. "My brother has a fast horse and buggy outside if you don't want to go through with this."

Everyone turned shocked gazes toward her. Rebecca pulled her hands from Mary's grip and fisted them on her hips. "Run away from Samuel on our wedding day? That would break his heart."

"I'm just offering." Emma rose from the bed and crossed to the window. "I think it's too late, anyway. The groom is here."

"He is?" Rebecca's heart leaped with joy as she hurried to her cousin's side. She scrubbed at the frost coating the inside of the glass and made a hole large enough to see out. Samuel, looking as handsome as ever, was gazing up at her from beside his buggy. He gave a jaunty wave and hurried inside the house.

"He doesn't look ready to run," Emma said as she elbowed Rebecca in the side.

"He looks very handsome today." Every time she saw Samuel, Rebecca was struck by how differently their lives might have turned out if not for God's intervention in the form of one terrible accident. Samuel's burns were completely healed, but he still bore patches of reddened skin on his cheeks and forehead. They didn't detract from his looks. Not in her eyes.

"Luke looks handsome, too," Emma said with a hint of sadness, then turned away from the window. Emma and Luke had gone out for a time before he left the Amish and got into trouble with the law. At the time, Emma had been heartbroken, but he wouldn't have been the right man for her. Everyone knew it.

Rebecca caught her lower lip between her teeth. Was she doing Samuel a disservice? Was there someone who would be better suited to be his wife? She had to be sure she was doing the right thing for him and not just because she wanted to be his wife. Downstairs, the strains of the first hymn rose in reverent recognition of the solemn occasion. Marriage was forever.

"Time to go." Mary took Rebecca's hand and led her toward the door and the crowd of family and friends waiting below.

Outside her door, Bishop Beachy stood waiting for her with Samuel at his side. Her heart skipped a beat, and then thudded into a wild gallop at the sight of her beloved's tender smile.

"If you two will follow me, I have a few words I share with all the couples I marry." The bishop turned and walked down the hall toward a smaller bedroom that had been prepared for the counseling by adding a little table and three chairs.

Rebecca started to follow him, but Samuel stopped her with a hand on her arm. "I haven't given you my engagement present yet."

Amish brides typically received small gifts from their intendeds when they agreed to wed. "A gift is not necessary, Samuel."

"I know, but I wanted you to have this." He pulled a packet from inside his vest and handed it to her.

Rebecca pulled away the paper to reveal a tiny cedar box. The hinges were smaller than any she had seen. The top was carved with the scene of a single raindrop striking the surface of the water, spreading ripples in all directions. The details were amazing. "Samuel, it's beautiful."

"Like you," he said softly.

She touched the delicate carving with her fingertips. "I adore it. *Danki.*"

He lifted her chin with his hand so she had to look at him. "I chose cedar because I know it will always remind you of the man you loved before me. I know he holds a special place in your heart. The water drop is because you have quenched the thirst in my soul I didn't know existed until I met you, and because you threw water on a sick man."

"Sprinkled, Samuel. I sprinkled water on you. You're never going to let that go, are you?" He could make her laugh even when she was nervous, and she loved that about him.

"Never. The rings in the water are the goodness that radiates from you toward everyone you touch. God willing, those ripples will spread to our children and grandchildren and for future generations untold. I'm so very blessed that you agreed to marry me. I will be the best husband and father that I can be. I promise you that."

Smiling at him, every reservation floated away from her heart and mind. They were meant for each other. Who was she to doubt the goodness of the Lord? She glanced down the hall to make sure the bishop wasn't looking, then she rose on tiptoe and planted a kiss on Samuel's lips.

"Save that until after the wedding, children," the bishop said from the end of the hall. His voice held only mild disapproval, but his face was set in stern lines.

Rebecca smothered a grin and saw Samuel do the same. He winked and said, "Let's get this over with. I have a lifetime of free kisses I'm holding for you."

She walked down the hall ahead of Samuel, confident that she was the woman God had chosen for him. She would never doubt it again.

* * * * *

Dear Reader,

I hope you enjoyed getting to know the Bowman family. I have a story planned for each brother. They all deserve someone special to love. It should be fun finding the right women for them.

Luke will be the star of my next book. He's been a challenge to write from the start, and I'm sure he will continue to be that way. His ambivalent feelings about remaining Amish certainly make him an unusual hero. Will Rebecca's cousin Emma Swartzentruber be the one to make him mend his ways and help him see a clear path? I hope so, but I need to get to know her better before I decide.

It's always a joy to dig deep into my characters and find strengths they didn't know they possessed.

Thank you again for choosing to read my stories. With so many books to choose from, I'm honored you picked up one of mine.

Blessings,

Patricia Davids